Lady Lucy's Lover

Lady Lucy's Lover

Marion Chesney

G.K. Hall & Co. • Chivers Press
Waterville, Maine USA Bath, England

This Large Print edition is published by G.K. Hall & Co., USA and by Chivers Press, England.

Published in 2001 in the U.S. by arrangement with Lowenstein Associates, Inc.

Published in 2001 in the U.K. by arrangement with the author.

U.S. Hardcover 0-7838-9605-0 (Romance Series Edition)
U.K. Hardcover 0-7540-4734-2 (Chivers Large Print)
U.K. Softcover 0-7540-4735-0 (Camden Large Print)

The text of this Large Print edition is unabridged.
Other aspects of the book may vary from the original edition.

Set in 16 pt. Plantin by Myrna S. Raven.

Printed in the United States on permanent paper.

British Library Cataloguing-in-Publication Data available

Library of Congress Cataloging-in-Publication Data

Chesney, Marion.
    Lady Lucy's lover / Marion Chesney.
       p. cm.
    ISBN 0-7838-9605-0 (lg. print : hc : alk. paper)
    1. Large type books.   I. Title.

 PR6053.H4535 L33 2001
   823´.914—dc21   2001039478

TO MARION AND JOHN LESLIE
WITH LOVE

Chapter One

"But I don't *want* a lover. I am in love with my husband," said Lady Lucy, turning around from her escritoire and looking in amazement at her friend, Mrs. Ann Hartford.

"I find the suggestion outrageous," added Lucy, Marchioness of Standish, "coming as it does from a respectable matron like yourself!"

Mrs. Hartford fanned herself lazily and looked at her friend with amusement. "You are upset and distressed and jealous, Lucy," she said. "I would like to see that feckless husband of yours made to feel the same."

"Guy is *not* feckless," snapped Lady Lucy, beginning to sharpen a quill pen with unnecessary vigor, "and . . . and . . . furthermore, I do not discuss my husband with *anyone*. Even you, Ann."

She turned back to the desk so that Mrs. Hartford should not see the tears in her eyes, and said in a light voice, "We are going to the Courtlands' ball tonight. Will you be there?"

Ann gave a wry smile, answered in the affirmative, and then began to talk lightly of the latest *on-dits* and the latest fashions while Lady Lucy regained control of her emotions and was able to turn and face her friend once more.

All the while she was talking, Mrs. Hartford was studying her friend's pretty face. She and Lucy had grown up together on neighboring estates in Sussex. Ann, thin and gawky, and four years older than Lucy, had blossomed into a fashionable young lady and had soon become wed to Mr. Giles Hartford, a rich member of the untitled aristocracy. Lucy had married the year after when she had reached only her eighteenth birthday. Her choice had been the handsome Marquess of Standish. Worldly wise Ann had cautioned her friend that the Marquess had a reputation as a rake and gambler. But in the first flush of love, Lucy would not hear a word against her paragon.

The Marquess and Lucy had been married a little under a year and rumor had it that the wild Marquess was wilder than ever and had returned to the experienced arms of one of London's leading courtesans, Harriet Comfort. Lady Lucy, a sparkling sunny beauty with golden hair and wide blue eyes, had gradually changed.

The innocent candor of her expression had turned to one of hurt wariness. Her former carefree laughter was hardly ever heard and she increasingly made her appearance at the opera, the rout, or in the Park at the fashionable hour on her own.

But Lady Lucy had comforted herself and her pride with the thought that the world still probably viewed herself and her husband as a happily married couple, and Ann's remark about taking a lover had shocked her to the core. Was the disaster of her marriage so obvious? Had she become an object of pity?

She forced herself to chat as easily and lightly as she could, feeling all the while a lump rising in her throat. She had never before had any secrets from Ann, but Lucy would not gossip about her husband. To admit, even to Ann, that the marriage was on the rocks would somehow kill all hope.

At last, to Lucy's relief, Ann rose to take her leave. She impulsively kissed Lucy on the cheek and said, "You are a good girl, Lucy, and I love you dearly. You will always have a home with me and Giles, should you wish."

"La! I have a home in town here, a home in the country, a barn of a place in Yorkshire, and a hunting box in Leicester. I think I am well supplied with homes," said Lucy, trying to laugh but ending up on a pathetic little croak.

"I think you know what I mean," said Ann, suddenly serious. And with that, she moved from the room with all the lithe grace which had turned her angular body and bony face into that of a much-admired leader of London society.

With her departure, the house suddenly seemed very quiet.

Dust motes floated in the shafts of sunlight from the long windows overlooking Clarence Square. Lady Lucy stood for a moment studying her face in the greenish looking glass hung in a corner of the room. She could no longer tell whether she was pretty or not. At one time, she had delighted in her own beauty because it had brought her to the attention of Guy, the most dashing and handsome young man on the London scene. She had met him during her first Season and had been married before the Season was over.

Her parents, Mr. and Mrs. Hyde-Benton, had been delighted with the match . . . too delighted to counsel their daughter against marrying a young man with such a wild reputation. Mr. Hyde-Benton had been plain Mr. Hyde in his youth, and a struggling young barrister with very little money. It was whispered he had made his fortune gambling. Now he craved a foothold in the ranks of the aristocracy which simple money could not buy him. His wife shared his ambitions. Lucy had tried to hint only a bare month before that all was not well with her marriage, but her parents had looked so outraged at the very suggestion that an aristocrat could do any wrong that Lucy had given up the attempt.

Now Lucy wondered how she had failed her husband. What had driven him back to the arms of his mistress? In the early days, their lovemaking had been tumultuous and quick, the Marquess rolling over on his side and dropping off to sleep as soon as it was over. Lucy had been vaguely disappointed, but young enough to enjoy the affectionate attention of her young husband at balls and parties when they went out together.

On public occasions, he showed all the tenderness and sweetness towards her that mysteriously evaporated as soon as they were alone.

But she had been sure of his love.

And then little by little he had begun to slip away from her. The house and estates in the country were left neglected. Now another Season was about to begin and they had not left town, even for a day.

Lucy had seen the famous Harriet Comfort. Ann had pointed out that lady when she and Lucy were driving in the Park. The courtesan had looked more like a respectable *mondaine* matron than a member of the Fashionable Impure and that made it all seem harder to bear. An absolutely stunning beauty would have made matters easier to understand. But Harriet — with her correct clothes and her patrician nose and large, liquid, slightly protruding eyes — hardly seemed to have the face or figure to launch a thousand ships, let alone drive one young lord from his marriage bed.

Then there were the increasing amounts of unpaid bills which were stuffed carelessly into the pigeonholes of her husband's desk. Any suggestion that they might be paid was greeted with scorn by her husband, who was in the habit of pointing out that only common people paid their tradesmen's bills.

11

Their townhouse was beautifully furnished in the latest fashion. Thin spindly chairs straddled their rosewood legs across the pale blues and creams of oriental carpets. The upholstery was mostly of striped silk and the curtains at the windows were of heavy striped silk also. Every sofa was backless and striped. It was sometimes like living in an elegant silk cage, thought Lucy, who missed the unfashionable clutter of her Sussex family home.

And then there were the clocks. Everyone who had attended the wedding had given them a clock, it seemed, and they ticked busily away in the silence of the house.

Although the butler faithfully wound them every day, they never seemed to chime at the same time. The tall case clocks boomed sonorously, the little gilt ones tinkled, and the grim marble ones emitted silvery chimes. Yet all the chattering, ticking and tocking and whispering of the clocks seemed to intensify the silence, as if underlining the fact that time was flying, flying, flying and the master was always from home.

London was bewildering to a young matron who was not yet old enough to have acquired a protective veneer of town bronze. In this the new nineteenth century, the dissipations of the last seemed to be intensified, with many of the members of the ton being driven by boredom into eccentricity. Snobbery and exclusiveness were increasing. Almack's, those famous assembly rooms, was paramount, ruled by its ten great patronesses with a rod of iron. The round of fun, fighting, cock fights, bets, routs, operas, assemblies, and tarts was trodden industriously and lampooned ferociously by Rowlandson in his cartoons, and in other cartoons, notably "The Adventures of Tom and Jerry."

The clubs and the great political houses focused the intellectual, political, and fashionable worlds; Devonshire House for the Tories, Holland House for the Whigs.

The only sin was to be Found Out. Liaisons and affairs were permissible only if they were never brought to the notice of society or the press. Complaisant husbands often accepted their wives' illegitimate offspring as their own. Very few men were considerate enough to use contraceptives, the Marquess going so far as to tell his blushing bride that he supposed she would breed quite soon and those fine kid leather sheaths were disgusting and making love with one of them on was like taking a bath in your stockings.

But Lucy had not become pregnant. She longed for a child with all her heart, hoping that the birth of a boy and heir to the Marquess would surely make him settle down and become accustomed to the responsibilities of marriage.

The rattling of carriage wheels on the cobbles outside made Lucy fly to the window. Her husband had arrived home. But in what a condition!

He was being supported up the steps by two friends who were scarcely more sober than the Marquess himself. Lucy ran into the hall just as the butler opened the door.

The Marquess's friends were sober enough to register the outrage on the Marchioness's pretty face and unceremoniously dropped their bundle onto the tiles of the hall floor, making a stumbling, hasty departure. The butler snapped his fingers and two footmen came running forward to lift my lord from the floor and carry him to bed. Feet trailing on the ground, the Marquess was dragged across the hall, his arms around the shoulders of the footmen. He let out an inane giggle and looked slyly at his wife. "Bit foxed, my sweeting," he mumbled.

The footmen stood irresolute. "Take my lord upstairs and put him to bed," snapped Lucy, and, turning on her heel, she walked back into the drawing room and slammed the door.

Of course, he had come home drunk many times before, but never in the middle of the afternoon. After a while, Lucy began to chide herself for being missish. Her husband was behaving like any other man. Somehow, she, Lucy, had failed him as a wife, which was why he found it necessary to seek his pleasures elsewhere. She must make one tremendous effort to look as beautiful as possible at the Courtlands' ball. She would be loving and affectionate. She would charm him as she had done in the past, and their married life would become the way she had always dreamed it should be.

Lucy decided to take a nap to fortify herself for the social rigors of the night to come and by the time she fell asleep she had thoroughly made up her mind that she was a very hard-hearted and selfish wife indeed.

Did not all men drink to excess and gamble to excess? Only the other day, it was said that a man had collapsed in front of White's Club in St. James's and the members had crowded to the window and had immediately begun laying bets as to whether he would live or die. A pass-erby had suggested bleeding the poor man but had been howled down by the gamblers who protested that this would affect the fairness of the betting.

She remembered the Marquess as he had been during the brief period of their engagement — warm and loving and tender. And so with the resilient optimism of youth, Lady Lucy fell asleep, convinced she would awake to a different world and a different marriage.

It was very hard to accept the reality of the situation when she was at last dressed in a gown of sheerest muslin, embroidered with seed pearls and worn over a slip of white satin.

Her golden hair was parted on the left side with curls hanging down over the left cheek. Drop earrings of Roman pearls completed the ensemble. Her reflection in the long glass had told her that she was in looks. The brilliance of her blue eyes detracted from the insipidness of her fair coloring, for blonds were not considered fashionable. She had descended the stairs to the small Blue Saloon on the ground floor where she normally awaited her husband. But as the minutes added up to a whole half-hour and still he did not come, she began to feel anxious and dispatched the first footman with a message for my lord.

But it was the butler, Wilson, who returned with the intelligence that my lord was feeling a trifle *seedy* and requested that my lady should go to the ball without him. My lord would join my lady later.

Lucy's pretty pink mouth compressed into a hard line. She wanted to send Wilson back upstairs again bearing a few sharp and choice words but there was something about all butlers that intimidated Lady Lucy. Sometimes she toyed with the fantasy that there was a special manufactory for turning out butlers from the same mold: fat and pear-shaped with large white faces and large pouches under the eyes and a pervading aura of sheer disinterest in the vagaries of the human race.

So instead she said quietly, "Very well, Wilson, have the carriage brought around."

While she awaited the arrival of the carriage, Lucy crossed to the window and pulled aside the curtain and looked out.

How frightening and dark and violent

London seemed when one had to venture out alone.

The street lamps cast barely more than a glimmer over the surrounding gloom of the square. They were glass globes half filled with whale oil and with bits of cotton twist for wick.

The globes were black with dirt, for the lamplighters who were employed to look after them, to light them at dusk and extinguish them at midnight, were "a contingent of greasy clodhopping fellows" with filthy fingers, who seemed incapable of filling a lamp without spilling the oil onto the head of anyone passing under their ladder.

Across the street, in the mansion directly opposite, had lived Lady Cummings, who had died only the other day. The house of death was shuttered and curtained, its door knocker wrapped around with flannel; on the front doorstep, dressed from head to foot in black, his pale face looming like a disk in the flickering light of the street lamp before the house, stood a professional mute, miming the agonies of despair for sixpence an hour (Sundays extra).

Lucy let the curtain fall with a sigh. What a marvelous city London had seemed on her first Season. *Then* she had not noticed the danger or squalor, feeling secure and protected with her tall, gallant Marquess always at her side.

The golden days of their courtship flicked through her mind as the carriage rumbled on its way to the Courtlands' ball. The excitement of warm kisses, pressures of the hand, all leading to that magic moment on her wedding night when she surrendered to him entirely. Lucy bit her lip. It was hard to admit even now that what should have been the culminating moment of glory, the crown set on their romance, had turned out to be . . . well . . . disappointing. Of course, he had drunk a great deal at the wedding. Almost unbidden, Ann's slightly mocking voice sounded in her ears: "Why not take a lover, Lucy?"

But that was unthinkable. The first glory of their love would return. All she could do was to try to understand him and say nothing that would drive him further from his home.

A tear of a size and beauty to rival the drops of her earrings rolled slowly down her cheek and she impatiently brushed it away.

Lord and Lady Courtland received Lucy at the entrance to the ballroom. "Your husband is not with you?" said Lady Courtland, making it sound more like an accusation than a question.

"He is unfortunately detained, my lady," said Lucy, curtsying low. "He will join me presently."

She made her escape into the ballroom and joined Ann Hartford and her husband, Giles. Giles was small and plump in contrast to his wife's tall elegance. Ann tactfully restrained from commenting on the absence of the Marquess. "A very good start to the Season, Lucy," she murmured. "All the world and his wife are here. We even have the impeccable Mr. Brummell and the Prince Regent is to honor us with his presence."

Lucy fanned herself, for the ballroom was very hot, lit as it was by hundreds of wax candles. The Exclusives were well represented. It was in the nature of high society to exclude undesirables and in that respect Regency society was already unique in the determined way it went about exclusion.

The ton called itself exclusive, its members the Exclusives, its ruling principle exclusivism. Innumerable hedges were built against intruders, elaborate rules for membership and subrules were set up, for the whole mess of taboos and shibboleths was society's way of keeping that dreadful *ennui* at bay.

It was even unfashionable to be married in church ("one simply *dies* of cold") and the Marquess had advised his unsophisticated bride not to remind society that they had been married in one, albeit a country church. Married couples were not expected to remain faithful to each other. But then most of them did not marry for love. It was for the most part a business partnership — your lands added to my lands, your fortune to mine. But Lucy had believed, and still believed, in love. Her parents, for all their vagaries of fortune and their social climbing, undoubtedly cared for each other. Ann Hartford doted on her chubby Giles. And so she secretly held the brittle fashionables in contempt — the hungry women with their transparent gowns, swelling bosoms, and rouged cheeks who drifted restlessly from one lover to another.

Not all of the men at the ball favored Mr. Brummell's fashion in evening dress — blue coat, white cravat, and form-fitting tights showing a discreet length of striped silk stocking above a dancing pump. Some preferred the still-conventional fashion of knee breeches. Despite the iniquitous flour tax, many still wore their hair powdered and wore glittering jewels pinned indiscriminately about their person. Then there were the eccentrics like Henry Cope, filled with a morbid longing to attract attention. He wore only green suits and cravats and it was said he bought green furniture, had his rooms painted green, and excited the ridicule of the lampoonists;

> Green garters, green hose, and deny
>   it who can,
> The brains, too, are green, of this
>   green little man!

Then there was Lord Dudley and Ward, propping up a pillar and talking to himself at great length, causing the wits to say, "It is only Dudley talking to Ward as usual."

And then there was . . .

But before Lucy could examine the sudden breathless shock a single glimpse of a tall dark-haired man at the entrance to the card room had given her, a partner was bending over her hand and requesting her to join him in the country dance.

Lucy was popular, and only her very obvious love for her husband stopped many of the gentlemen from pursuing her. She was a great favorite as a dance partner because she danced beautifully and was guaranteed to say any number of charming and not too frighteningly intelligent things.

From time to time, she twisted her head, looking for that tall, dark man whose very presence had startled her in such a strange way, but she could see no sign of him in the ballroom and assumed that he must be in the card room.

She had just finished performing a lively reel with an ebullient young Hussar when she saw her husband. No longer did her heart beat faster with joy. Instead, all she felt was an apprehensive ache somewhere in the region of that organ.

His handsome high-nosed face was marred with patches of red and looked slightly swollen. His normally pale blue eyes were crisscrossed with red veins, and instead of smelling of new brandy, he smelled abominably of old spirits and snuff.

But all his famous charm was to the fore and he turned the full blast of it on his young wife.

"Lucy," he murmured, kissing her hand. "What a wretch you must think me, and what a forgiving little wife you are. We'll spend the whole day together tomorrow and I warrant I shall bring the stars back to your eyes. I know you've been cursing me for being a poor sort of husband, but I'll make it up to you. You do forgive me, sweeting, do you not?"

Lucy looked up into his anxious eyes and her heart melted.

"Of course I forgive you," she whispered. "Do you wish to dance?"

"No, my love. Food is what I need. Let us go and sample some refreshments."

He tucked her hand in his arm and led her to the refreshment room. The long windows were open to the garden and a cool breeze made a refreshing change from the heat of the ball-room.

He fetched her food and drink, hovering over her anxiously until she was seated and served, in such a humble, apologetic, almost school-boyish way that Lucy's heart went out to him.

"What have you planned for us to do tomorrow, Guy?" she asked gaily.

"Oh, tol rol, just drive somewhere, you know, and be by ourselves for a little."

"I would like that of all things," said Lucy earnestly. "I had . . . had begun to think you had ceased to care for me."

"Fustian. That beanpole friend of yours has been putting nasty ideas in your pretty head."

"Ann? Oh, no. It's just that . . . well, I may as well be open with you, Guy. There are terrible rumors that you are spending your time with Harriet Comfort."

The red patches on the Marquess's face deepened to an angry color. "Harriet Comfort is the fashion," he said in a calm voice, belied by the angry glint in his eyes. "One calls on her to take tea. It's a ritual thing like going to the opera or stuff like that. Even Brummell goes and no one has ever credited him with any mad passions."

"Oh," said Lucy in a small voice. "But people do talk so, Guy, and I would rather not share you with *anyone*."

"Don't listen to all those tabby cats. I won't go again. So there! Smile at me, my love. It's not like you to be such an angry kitten."

Lucy smiled and, as she did so, she had an uncomfortable feeling that she was being watched. She turned her head slightly and met the steady gaze of the tall, dark man who had disturbed her so much before. He was standing at the door to the refreshment room, talking to three ladies while his eyes ranged over their heads to where Lucy was sitting with her husband.

He had thick black hair worn in a fashionable Brutus crop and strange gray eyes which were almost silver. His heavy lids gave his face a shuttered appearance. His skin was very white and the Greek classicism of his face was saved from effeminate perfection by the strength of his chin and the long humorous curve of his mouth. His evening coat was tailored to fit across his broad shoulders without a wrinkle and his knee breeches and clocked stockings were molded to a pair of long, muscular legs.

He was a very imposing man, handsome in an autocratic way. Lucy lowered her eyes quickly, feeling to her confusion a blush mounting to her cheek.

"Who is that tall man over there?" she whispered to the Marquess.

He followed the wave of her fan and his eyes lit up. " 'Fore George! That's Habard — Simon, the tenth Duke. He'll put us all in the shade. I wonder what brings him to Town. He hardly ever does the Season."

"Is he married?" asked Lucy, fanning her hot cheeks.

"Not he! Too clever to be leg-shackled," laughed the Marquess as Lucy winced.

"And is it his bachelor state that puts you all in the shade?" asked Lucy quickly to cover her hurt.

"No. Habard's an out-and-outer. Up to every rig and row in town. A top-of-the-trees. Can pop one over Jackson's guard and can drive better than Lade."

"Hush!" said Lucy, putting a stop to this flow of enthusiastic cant by laying a restraining hand on her husband's sleeve. "His Grace is coming this way. I think Lady Courtland is going to introduce us."

The Marquess and Marchioness of Standish rose to their feet. "His Grace the Duke of Habard wishes to make the acquaintance of your beautiful wife," said Lady Courtland. "Your Grace, allow me to present the Marquess and Marchioness of Standish. Lady Standish, His Grace the Duke of Habard, Lord Standish, His Grace the Duke of Habard." And then looking quite fatigued with all the exertion of the introductions, Lady Courtland gave a little half-bow from the waist and took her leave.

"Pray be seated," said the Duke with a wave of his hand. He smiled suddenly and blindingly at Lucy, who sat down feeling quite weak at the knees.

The Duke drew up a chair between the Marquess and Lucy. "I say, another bottle of burgundy!" shouted the Marquess to a passing footman. "This is a great honor, Habard," he said with all the enthusiasm of a schoolboy. "We did meet, you know, some years back . . . at Codlingham's shoot, I think it was."

The Duke nodded, studying Lucy's lowered eyes.

"And what brings you to Town?" went on the Marquess jovially. "We are not often honored with your presence."

"I have had a great deal to do in the country," said the Duke. His voice was deep and husky. "I have no intention of letting my estates go to rack and ruin. How are matters at Standish? Do you expect a good harvest?"

"We . . . we don't know," said Lucy. "We have not been there . . . oh, since we became married."

This naive remark earned her a burning look of irritation from her husband.

"These young brides," he said with a smile that did not meet his eyes. "You know how it is, Habard. She would make me out to be an absentee landlord."

"In your case, Standish," said the Duke gallantly, "it would be understandable if you were. The delights of town and the delights of a pretty bride —"

"But you do not answer my question," interrupted the Marquess. "What brings you to Town?"

"Oh, a need to see a beautiful face once in a while," said the Duke. "My farming work does not qualify me for the role of monk, would you say, Lady Standish?"

"I-I have no idea, Your Grace."

"I plan to visit Jackson's tomorrow, Habard, and would be honored to see you in action," said the Marquess, helping himself liberally to burgundy. Gentleman Jackson's boxing saloon was a haunt of the Corinthians, the bucks and bloods and Toms and Jerrys who aspired to be expert in all forms of sport.

"But . . . but . . ." began Lucy and then flushed and bit her lip.

"You were about to say, Lady Standish?"

"Nothing," muttered Lucy, but casting a fulminating look at the Marquess. Had he forgotten so soon that they were to spend the day together?

"I am president for the day at the general meeting of archers at Blackheath," said the Duke. "I would be honored if you would both be my guests. But perhaps you do not have an interest in archery . . . ?"

"Oh, indeed we do, don't we, Lucy," said the Marquess, giving his bride a warning scowl.

"Yes, indeed," said Lucy faintly.

"It is an early start, I am afraid. I shall call for you at ten in the morning. Clarence Square, I believe?"

"That's exceeding cordial of you, ain't it, Lucy?" said the Marquess.

"Not at all. Now if you will excuse me?"

The Duke stood up and took his leave.

Lucy rounded on her husband. "You said we should spend tomorrow together."

"Look here, Lucy," said the Marquess angrily. "When an out-and-outer like Habard singles you out, you don't turn down his invitation."

"But you said . . ."

"I said, *I said*," jeered the Marquess. Lucy's eyes filled with tears. "Oh, if you're about to play the watering-pot, I'm going."

And with that, the Marquess rose abruptly to his feet, nearly sending the chair flying, and stalked off.

The Marquess was quite restored to good

humor after he had bragged of the forthcoming outing to several of his cronies. It was no small thing to be known to be on comfortable terms with a paragon like the Duke.

After some time, he bethought himself of his wife. The Duke had seemed to find Lucy pretty and it would not do his standing in the Duke's eyes any good if he were seen to be at odds with his wife.

He decided to seek her out to make amends but she was dancing a lengthy country dance with a young man.

The Marquess was still feeling too fragile to take part in the dance himself so he propped up a pillar under the musicians' gallery and waited for the country dance to end.

It was then that he heard the Duke's voice coming from the other side of the pillar. The man the Duke was with asked loudly, "And how did you find the Standishes?"

"Oh, very well," came the Duke's lazy, husky voice, and the Marquess preened.

"But," the Duke went on with quite dreadful clarity, "I would not have given either of 'em the time of day. He is a boor and she is a timid little mouse, but I promised Ann Hartford to be civil to them. I'm taking them with me to that archery contest at Blackheath and after I have paid my promises to Mrs. Hartford, with good luck, I may not have to trouble myself with either of them again."

The red patches on the Marquess's face

deepened almost to purple. He moved away quickly so that he would not be discovered. He writhed under the insult and yet he bitterly longed for Habard's friendship.

His friends had promised to attend the archery contest. And so he simply must go. He longed to confide his woes to a sympathetic ear. Lucy would simply say that they must not go and that they must have nothing to do with the Duke again.

She was *so* unsophisticated. And damn Ann Hartford for her patronizing ways, always poking her long nose into his affairs.

All he needed was a little feminine comfort and understanding.

Comfort.

All at once he thought longingly of Harriet. Harriet who understood better than anyone the trials and tribulations of a fashionable man.

Harriet had so far favored him above her other courtiers. That had made him envied and the Marquess needed to be envied. The fashionable life of London consumed him. It meant all the world to him. To be seen, to be noticed, to be envied — that was what he craved.

And that was what Lucy did not understand. The hold Harriet Comfort had over her husband was fashionable rather than sexual.

He blundered his way through the ballroom to the exit and found himself face to face with Ann Hartford.

"Ah, just the lady I was looking for," he said

cheerfully. "Do tell my wife, Mrs. Hartford, that I have the headache and must leave. Lucy will understand. She is having such fun t'would be a pity to spoil her pleasure."

"Being abandoned by her husband is the only thing that is likely to spoil her pleasure," said Ann tartly, but the Marquess smiled vaguely, affected not to hear, and took his leave.

When the country dance finished, Ann conveyed the Marquess's message to Lucy, bitterly watching the hurt and dismay in her friend's wide eyes.

"Then I had better go too," said Lucy.

"Tish!" exclaimed Ann. "Habard! My Lord Duke. My friend Lady Standish is threatening to leave us, and all because my lord has left with the headache."

Lucy found the Duke's eyes on her, strangely cool and calculating.

"I must go," she said nervously. "Please do not try to detain me."

The Duke bowed in indifferent acquiescence to her wishes and Ann sighed as Lucy hurried off.

Lucy could hardly wait to get home. She was consumed with guilt. It seemed to her now that her husband had every right to be furious with her. She had corrected him in front of the Duke, had made him sound like an absentee landlord. And she had sworn to be loving and gay and affectionate.

She decided, boldly, to go to her husband's bedroom as soon as she got home. He had obviously left on foot or had taken a sedan, since he had at least, thoughtfully, left the carriage for her. Poor Lucy did not for a minute realize her husband's "thoughtfulness" was simply prompted by a desire not to let the household servants know where he was spending the night.

She ran lightly up the stairs to her husband's bedroom and knocked at the door. Only the silence of the house answered her, a silence punctuated by the ticking and tocking and chiming of the many clocks.

She opened the door very gently. An oil lamp was burning on the toilet table. The bed curtains were drawn back and my lord's nightshirt was laid out on the bed.

But of the Marquess there was no sign.

Lucy went quickly to her room and went slowly to bed after telling her maid to awaken her early.

Her mind refused to think. Worn out and exhausted with emotion, she immediately fell asleep.

Chapter Two

Lucy could not help hoping for a new start to her marriage as her maid helped her to dress in the morning.

The sun was shining down outside and the little square of sky she could see from her window was the same celestial blue as her cambric gown.

The dress was one of her favorites, having a double row of shell lace at the neck and wrists. It was high-waisted in the current mode, with a broad blue silk ribbon tied under the bosom and meeting in a bow at the back. White linen gloves, an amber necklace, a blue parasol, and a white chip bonnet completed the ensemble.

She refused to think about the ball, or even about the Duke of Habard. It was an outing, and she and her husband would at least be, in part, together.

But Wilson, the butler, informed her as my lady descended the stairs that my lord was not at home and had sent no message.

"Very good, Wilson," said Lucy flatly and went into the drawing room, standing with her back to the door until the butler quietly closed it behind her.

Lucy wondered sadly if butlers ever knew how many "very goods" covered so many infinite depths of grief and sorrow. She felt small and unattractive and insignificant, and the face that stared back at her from the glass looked pinched and white. She decided she would tell Wilson to inform the Duke of Habard that my lord and my lady were indisposed. But a barrel organ in the square was playing a jaunty tune, and a warm breeze holding all the scents of spring and the promise of summer to come drifted in at the window. A little spark of rebellion began to burn in Lucy's heart. He should *not* find her meekly waiting if and when he returned home. She would go after all.

She felt so low in spirits that when the clocks in their jumbled way began to chime ten o'clock, she had quite decided that the Duke of Habard would not come either.

But the door of the drawing room opened and Wilson announced portentously that His Grace, The Duke of Habard, was awaiting my lord and my lady outside, not wanting to leave his cattle as the team was very fresh, and that he, Wilson, had not seen fit to inform His Grace that my lord was not at home.

"You did very well, Wilson," said Lucy, picking up her diamond-shaped reticule. "You may inform my lord when he returns that I have gone ahead to Blackheath."

Two tall footmen followed her from the house and assisted her into the Duke's high-perched phaeton.

The Duke gave Lucy a quiet "good morning"

and immediately set his team in motion.

"I am afraid my husband is indisposed," said Lucy, rather startled at the Duke's lack of interest in the whereabouts of the Marquess.

"Indeed," said the Duke indifferently. "It is a fine morning, Lady Standish. I am going to set a fair pace once we are clear of the press of traffic, so I shall not be able to indulge much in conversation until we arrive."

Lucy nodded, content after all her emotional turmoil to simply enjoy the drive without being obliged to talk.

She covertly studied the Duke's profile from under the brim of her hat, noticing the strength of his chin and the way his heavy lids half veiled his eyes. He wore a curly brimmed beaver, a blue coat with silver buttons, leather breeches, and glossy Hessian boots.

He turned suddenly and smiled down at her, a smile of singular sweetness, and Lucy's heart thudded against her ribs almost as if she had received a fright.

They drove south over the river, gradually picking up speed along the Old Kent Road, over the Grand Surrey Canal which sparkled in the bright sunlight, past Hatcham House, and through New Cross. At Loam Pit Hill, he slackened the pace and remarked that they were well ahead of time.

"Does your husband know of a certain Mr. Barrington?" he asked abruptly, slowing his team to a canter.

"I have never heard him speak of such a gentleman," said Lucy.

"Well, Mr. Barrington is a financier who buys up bills of exchange." He smiled a little at the blank look on Lucy's face. "A bill of exchange is a written acknowledgment of the existence of a debt, Lady Standish."

"Oh, IOU's," said Lucy, her face clearing.

"Yes. Say your husband gave such a bill of exchange to his tailor, the tailor may then use that bill or IOU to pay for cloth. The clothmaker may use the bill to pay for raw materials and so on, and sometimes the bill can pass through a hundred hands."

"I don't see how this concerns my husband."

"I am only giving you a timely warning to pass on to him. Now, often a financier will buy some of these bills as an investment. As he loses his use of the money until the date of payment — usually three months for London bills — he charges interest. This interest is known as "discount" and can be very high. I am not only warning your husband. I have passed on this warning to many young men. Barrington specializes in securing the bills of any aristocrat whose land he covets.

"This Barrington is a Yorkshire man who cultivates a bluff, fatherly manner. He makes it appear, without precisely saying so, that he will not press for payment on the exact date. But he does. And he charges very high interest. It is not only land he wants, but power. So far as I

35

know, no influential people have fallen into his clutches, but there are unsavory rumors circulating about his practices."

Lucy thought guiltily of the rolls of unpaid bills stuffed into the pigeonholes of her husband's desk. But they were small household bills, dressmakers bills, tailors bills, nothing she was sure that came to very much.

"Thank you, Your Grace," she said demurely.

"And tell me about yourself, Lady Standish," he went on. "Shall I have the pleasure of seeing you about Town this Season?"

"Oh, yes," said Lucy, unaware that she sighed as she spoke. "We shall go to all the routs and ton parties, and the theater and the opera."

"And how terribly sad it all is," he mocked.

"Your Grace!"

"You make it sound like a catalogue of terrible, burdensome duties."

"Oh, no. I did not mean to sound like that *at all*. I am merely depressed because my poor husband is indisposed."

"Ah, yes, I had forgot. What is the nature of his indisposition?"

"A recurring trouble," said Lucy repressively, while the Duke stole her a sidelong look. He wondered whether this little Marchioness was aware that her husband's "recurring trouble" might be Harriet Comfort.

"Are you at all interested in archery?" asked the Duke to change the subject.

"I do not know. I am not acquainted with the sport."

"It is very fashionable among the ladies. Perhaps today will inspire you. I am going to spring my horses again, so hold on tightly."

Once more houses and cottages and fields raced past as the miles to Blackheath flashed by under the huge yellow wheels of the phaeton.

Lucy's worries began to fade away before a feeling of exhilaration. If only Guy were here! How he would have admired the Duke's driving!

Then Lucy began to wonder why the Duke had chosen to bring his phaeton, which was clearly built only to seat two, and he did not seem at all like the sort of gentleman who would neglect the comfort of his guests.

"Blackheath!" said the Duke, slowing once more and pointing with his whip.

Six huge marquees had been raised on the heath, their colorful banners fluttering in the breeze.

"It is perhaps as well my husband did not join us or we would have been sorely crushed on the journey," said Lucy.

"I must have had a premonition he would not come," answered the Duke calmly. "Do you know who is competing?"

Lucy shook her head.

"Quite an assembly. The Royal Surrey Bowmen, Saint George's Bowmen, Royal Kentish Bowmen, the Toxophilites, Woodmen of Arden, Robin Hood's Bowmen, Bowmen of Chevy Chase, and the Suffolk Bowmen. I hope you had a good breakfast, Lady Standish. We do not break for refreshments until three."

Lucy had been too upset to eat any breakfast at all and was already extremely hungry with all the fresh air, but she murmured that she had indeed eaten.

There was already quite a large crowd there. After they had alighted from the carriage, they were led to the judging stand by the Earl of Avelsford. For the very first time, Lucy became aware of the Duke's importance and popularity. Men bowed and women curtsied — the latter flashing Lucy envious glances.

The Duke made no excuse for the Marquess's absence, nor was asked for any, Lucy noticed with a queer little pang.

To Lucy's surprise and relief, the Duke did not ogle any of the very pretty women around — the Marquess had assured her that all gentlemen did this — but settled down comfortably next to her on the stand and began to explain which team of archers was which. The team of archers with a banner depicting three arrows surrounded with an oak wreath was Robin Hood's Bowmen, and the sable field between a chevron and charged with bugle horns and three silver arrows belonged to the Toxophilites.

It was extremely flattering to Lucy to find that her companion seemed perfectly happy to devote his whole attention to her entertainment and comfort. Her large eyes began to sparkle and a faint rose mantled her normally pale face.

She almost managed to forget just how hungry she was until the archery contest broke at three o'clock for refreshments. It was only a half-hour break but thanks to the Duke's eminent position and thoughtfulness, she was amply provided with tea and sandwiches and lemonade.

Then when the band in the middle of the heath struck up "The Girl I Left Behind Me" as a signal that the contest was about to resume, she thought guiltily about her husband and wondered for almost the first time in several hours what he was doing.

The Marquess had had an exhausting night — not in the arms of his mistress, but waiting below stairs until she should finish passing the night in the arms of one of her other lovers. Instead of sleeping, he passed the night playing solitaire and drinking, reluctant to leave this slim mansion in Manchester Square which he found strangely soothing.

He was just falling into an uneasy sleep as the gray light of dawn filtered through the shutters when a maid arrived with the intelligence that the mistress would see him now.

Immediately awake, he mounted the stairs to Harriet's boudoir two at a time. To his relief she was alone, sitting in front of the dressing table, brushing her long brown hair.

Words tumbled one over the other as he explained the Duke's insult, how he felt he should not go to Blackheath, but on the other hand longing to be seen in the Duke's company.

And Harriet took his hand in her own and soothingly told him that everyone who was anyone in society insulted people behind their backs. It was the way of the world. She invented quite staggering and fictitious insults that had been endured with fortitude by such famous people as Beau Brummell and Lord Alvanley, speaking in her soft, well-modulated voice while he hung eagerly on her every word. He should go to Blackheath, advised Harriet, but a little late. His "little wife" would not mind traveling on her own with the Duke. Harriet in fact secretly enjoyed her power over the Marquess. She felt it did her reputation as a *femme fatale* no harm to be seen luring this young Marquess away from the bedchamber of his pretty bride.

"I have so many worries that Lucy does not understand," complained the Marquess. "She does not realise the vast expense it takes to be fashionable. I am heading for dun territory, Harriet, and don't know quite how I am to come about."

"You have plenty of property," said Harriet, raising her pencilled eyebrows. "You have a place in Yorkshire, I believe, that you never visit. Sell it!"

"Sell!" exclaimed the Marquess. He withdrew his hands. "You do not understand us, Harriet. We do not sell our property."

Harriet lowered her eyes to mask her irritation.

She knew the Marquess was not using the "Royal we." He meant that she, the commoner, did not understand "we," the aristocrats.

"I am merely trying to be practical," she said levelly. "But I should have remembered that all the Exclusives go to Mr. Barrington."

"Yes, of course," said the Marquess, who did not want to betray for a moment that he did not know of whom she was speaking. "Ah, yes, good old Barrington."

"Yes," murmured Harriet sweetly, "the bill broker. Such a seedy little office in Fetter Lane, but so understanding and so generous. . . ."

"Quite," said the Marquess, making a firm mental note of the name.

"And now," said Harriet soothingly. "You must lie down for a little or you will not look your best at the archery contest. . . ."

Lucy was beginning to feel sleepy. A stiff warm breeze had sprung up, snapping the banners above the marquees and sending the dresses of the ladies billowing out.

The crowd had become immense, sometimes pushing forward across the line of the targets, and there were a few awful moments when it seemed as if a spectator must surely be impaled by an arrow.

The motley crowd of entertainers which seemed to appear by magic at any large gathering was very much in evidence.

A half-naked man was demonstrating how he could roll his back on broken bottles and emerge unscathed. A bear ward was beating his drum, his large, shaggy animal stumbling behind him. A juggler was tossing silver balls up into the air and chapmen were selling pins and ribbons.

At last it was six o'clock and the band began to play to signal the end of the tournament. The Earl of Avelsford, with the stewards, collected the target papers, and went into a huddle around the Duke of Habard, who had crossed the grass to meet them. After some deliberation, the prize was declared in favor of Dr. Leith of Greenwich, captain of target of the Royal Kentish Bowmen, for having split the central mark of the goal at a distance of 100 yards.

The Duke presented the prize to the much-excited and flushed doctor, and then the other prizes to the runners-up. Mr. Anderson, captain of numbers of Robin Hood's Bowmen, who came in third, was just as excited and stammered his thanks to the Duke and offered his best wishes "to the fair Duchess." To Lucy's confusion, the Duke smiled blandly and did not correct him.

Lucy turned to thank the Duke for a pleasant

day since she assumed they would be returning to London immediately, but the Duke looked down at her and said, "We sit down to dinner at Willis's Rooms in Blackheath at eight o'clock. I engaged a private parlor for you at the Tub of Butter Inn, since I thought you would like to rest for a little before the celebrations."

"But my husband . . . ?" began Lucy.

"Ah, I had forgot. Very ill, is he?"

"Well, not exactly. You see . . ."

"In that case, I see no reason why you cannot enjoy your dinner first. Unless, of course, you think he is waiting impatiently for you at home?"

Lucy had a sudden picture of scrambling home only to find an empty house. Her face hardened. She would stay. But somewhere inside she was beginning to dread what her husband would say. And then it seemed quite terrible that she should dread anything about the man she loved so much.

"Thank you," she replied. "You have gone to a great deal of trouble on my behalf, Your Grace."

He merely smiled and began to lead her through the crowd towards his phaeton, stopping now and then to talk to his friends and to introduce her. He managed to convey a subtle atmosphere which implied that he was proud of her company. Lucy reflected wryly that he must be well mannered inside as well as out.

At one point when the dispersing crowd was shoving past in all directions, she stumbled against him and he quickly put an arm around her shoulders to steady her. The effect of his touch was startling, to say the least. It seemed as if her whole body had begun to throb. He quickly dropped his arm and Lucy blushed, wondering if these odd tumultuous feelings coursing through her body had been transmitted to him.

She was glad to retire to the private luxury of a bedroom and private parlor at the inn. The Duke promised to call for her at seven-thirty. After he had left, she glanced at the little watch pinned to her bosom. Quarter to seven! She dared not lie down on that inviting bed and go to sleep.

She contented herself by rearranging her hair and bathing her face and arms. Then she opened the latticed window and looked out.

The window overlooked a square of garden at the back with a few rustic chairs and tables. A lilac tree, heavy with blossom, stood gracefully in the shadow of a mellow old wall. A flowerbed was glowing in the late evening light with a jumble of flowers. The breeze had died and the air was still and sweet.

She leaned her elbows on the sill and let the peace of the evening seep into her bones. And then, unbidden, came that old yearning feeling, that longing for the innocent days of her courtship. She remembered one golden day, walking through the gardens at her family home, hand in hand with Guy. The feel of his hand holding her own had set her trembling with anticipation and excitement. And yet no adventures of the marriage bed had ever been able to conjure up in her the sexual sweetness of that simple contact. Of course, friends other than Ann Hartford had warned her of the Marquess's rakehell life. But he had seemed so much in love with her, so *sweetly* in love.

It had been exciting planning the redecoration of the townhouse in London, yet when it had been completed, not one of her suggestions had been followed. Everything was new and fashionable and characterless.

The Marquess always talked at great length about what and who were fashionable and what and who were not.

He had a sister, Georgina, who rarely came to town.

But one day when they had been walking along Piccadilly, Lucy had seen Georgina coming towards them, accompanied by her maid.

"There's Georgina, Guy," she had cried.

" 'Fore George!" her husband had hissed. "Don't she look a frump. Cut her, Lucy!"

And Lucy, too amazed to do other than obey her husband, had affected not to see Georgina, who was left looking after them and calling her brother's name in a loud, amazed voice.

"It's quite the thing," Guy had assured her.

"Brummell cut his brother when the fellow appeared in Town wearing country clothes."

But the Duke of Habard was fashionable, reflected Lucy, and he did not seem to cut anyone. He was equally pleasant to everybody. This seemed a very treacherous thought, so Lucy twisted a curl in her finger, and dreamed of her marriage returning to its first glory.

When a knock came at the door, she whirled around, her mind full of Guy, young and eager, as he had been only a little under a year ago in the sunny days of their courtship.

She ran lightly across the room and swung open the door, her husband's name dying on her lips.

The Duke looked enigmatically down at the face below his, which had for a brief second blazed with warmth and love and yearning. The next instant, she had lowered her eyes and said in a slightly shaky voice, "I am ready to go, Your Grace."

As she moved to pick up her reticule, she noticed that a tray of refreshments was laid out in the private parlor adjoining the bedroom and was now destined to remain untouched — by Lucy at least. No doubt the inn's servants would be grateful to my lady for her forgetfulness.

The Duke talked easily and urbanely as they walked down the stairs and out again to his carriage. But all the while, he was thinking of that brief, blazing, passionate transformation and could not help cursing the absent Marquess. No doubt Harriet Comfort had kept her claws firmly embedded in his flesh.

Willis's Rooms were crowded and the dinner was almost informal in its jollity. Lucy sat at the head table, facing the room, with the Duke at her side, uneasily aware she was being awarded all the courtesies which would normally have been offered to his Duchess, had he been married. The Duke rose before the dinner and made a short, brief, witty speech and then sat down to loud applause.

And then all at once the Marquess was there, flushed and schoolboyish, pulling up a chair without waiting for permission and placing himself between the Duke and Lucy.

He immediately turned to the Duke and started to babble out fulsome apologies. He had been delayed in Town on business matters and the pole of his carriage had broken on the road to Blackheath and . . .

The Duke firmly and pleasantly cut short the Marquess's apologies. "I am glad to see you well, Standish," he said, "for I was informed by your wife that you were suffering from a recurring problem. But if you will find a place at my other side, I will be able to pay better attention to you. Of course, you will wish to make your most humble apologies to your wife, although I am grateful to you. I cannot say in all honesty that your company was missed, for it is a long time since I spent the day in such delightful company."

"What! Heh, yes o'course. Sorry, Lucy." The Marquess drew up a chair on the other side of the Duke. The Duke turned his attention to Lucy and began to talk to her quietly about the various people in the rooms.

The Marquess fretted, trying unsuccessfully from time to time to attract the Duke's attention to himself.

It was damnable of Harriet to let him sleep so late and then to laugh at him. But what would he do without her? This Barrington appeared to be a friend of hers and she had promised to take him to meet Barrington on the morrow. That way all his bills and troubles would be taken care of.

After the toasts, the conversation became more noisy and general. The Marquess had drunk quickly and steadily and now found he had the courage to break in on the Duke's conversation with Lucy.

"I say," he said loudly, "I heard the most vastly amusing *on-dit*."

The Duke politely turned to the Marquess and raised one eyebrow. It was all the encouragement the Marquess needed.

"Well, it appears," he began very loudly, "that a certain Duke of V. and his Duchess were traveling in Sussex. They stopped at this inn. The landlord was a very surly fellow and the Duke told him if he did not improve his manner he would haul him before a justice of the peace. But the landlord did not correct his manner. 'By Gad,' says the Duke to the Duchess, 'I've a good mind to bring out my *dedimus* right now.' 'Oh, if you must, you must,' says the Duchess wearily. 'But can't you wait until this fellow leaves the bedroom'?"

And the Marquess leaned back in his chair and laughed loud and long at his own joke. Then he realized the Duke was looking at him with an expressionless face and Lucy with a puzzled one.

"What does *dedimus* mean?" asked Lucy, leaning slightly across the Duke.

"Well, hey, *dedimus* is a sort of right to act as your own Justice of the Peace. But don't you see, *that's* not what the Duchess thought he was going to take out."

"Have some more wine, Standish," said the Duke in freezing accents.

"Very good of you, sir. Oh, *Lucy*. You're such a widgeon. You still don't understand. What does a man take out when he's about to make love to a woman?"

"Oh, I see," said Lucy, shrinking back so that the Duke's tall figure blocked her from her husband's view. She was embarrassed, desperately embarrassed for Guy. His voice had been very loud and penetrating and several of the ladies were looking at him in disdain. Then when she had leaned forward to ask him that question, her bosom had brushed against the Duke's arm, and a whole thunderclap of tumultuous sensations had been added to the one of embarrassment.

Guy rallied magnificently. He stopped drinking anything stronger than lemonade. He asked the Duke quiet, polite questions about who was running at Newmarket, and what were the prospects of the latest pugilist, and could he hope to rival Mendoza or Cribb.

He threw an occasional affectionate, teasing remark to Lucy. The Duke began to thaw visibly. Standish was a charming fellow after all. It was a pity he could not be more faithful to his wife, but then, who was?

The Duke found himself, however, becoming slightly intrigued by Lucy Standish. He could not think why she had seemed so colorless to him at the ball. She was young and bashful and occasionally gauche. But when she was happy as she was now, she outshone any other woman in the room. And then an image of Lucy, shining and passionate and yearning as she had been when she had opened the bedroom door of the inn, thinking that he was her husband, came back to him, and all at once he felt unaccountably sad and wished to be rid of the Standishes as soon as possible.

And so it was the Marquess who drove Lucy back to town under a small, pale, late spring moon. She fell asleep very quickly, her head on his shoulder, and he felt quite a rush of tenderness towards her.

After all, if such a Notable as Habard found

Lucy attractive, then it would do his own social position no harm to be seen to be paying a little more attention to his wife!

Chapter Three

"You were quite right to come to me, Lord Standish," said Mr. Barrington jovially.

The Marquess began to relax visibly. Mr. Barrington's office was admittedly a bit dirty and seedy and there had been a few suspicious-looking characters hovering around in the street outside, but Mr. Barrington himself had quickly dispelled any sinister first impressions caused by his place of business.

He looked more like a Yorkshire farmer than a bill broker. He wore an old-fashioned bag wig set slightly askew on his large round head. His cheeks were round and ruddy and his small eyes were very blue and twinkling. He was wearing an old single-breasted militia coat deprived of its facings and trappings, over a short, sort of shriveled-up waistcoat, old white mole-skin breeches, and hessians badly in need of some Warring's blacking.

Harriet Comfort had taken a chair over in the corner by the window and appeared to divorce herself from the proceedings.

"All you do, my lord," went on Mr. Barrington, "is to get all your creditors to send me your bills of exchange and that way a gentleman like yourself will not be plagued with duns at his door. Of course, I am a businessman and, should your bills go over the limit, well, I do charge a bit of interest. But I am not a pressing man, not a pressing man."

"It's very good of you," said the Marquess.

"Not at all. Not at all. Your parents are dead, my lord? Sad. And your uncle, the Duke of Hardhamshire would not, I gather, help you out of any . . . er . . . financial embarrassment?"

"Good Gracious! No! He's a tartar. A martinet. He doesn't understand that one must keep a good table and dress well and . . . and . . ."

"And gamble, my lord? You dropped ten thousand pounds at Watier's the other night."

"You are well informed," said the Marquess haughtily.

"But I am generous to young men in bad financial straits, my lord."

"I do not see why you should be," remarked the Marquess, becoming suspicious.

"Well, I shall tell you, although it pains me deeply. I had a son who was very wild. He played deep and got into the River Tick and appealed to me to pull him out. I told him he was old enough to stand on his own feet. He . . . he . . . blew his brains out."

A tear escaped from one of Mr. Barrington's blue eyes and rolled down one plump, rosy cheek. The Marquess looked down in sudden embarrassment.

"I . . . I have his miniature here," said Mr. Barrington, fumbling in a capacious pocket. He handed the small case over to the Marquess, who opened it up. It was a portrait of a handsome youth with large girlish eyes and a sensitive mouth. He had, in fact, blown his brains out — but he was not Mr. Barrington's son but one of his late creditors.

"So you see," said Mr. Barrington, pausing to blow his nose on a large handkerchief, "that explains my concern."

The Marquess nodded and tried to look sympathetic — although now that Mr. Barrington had established his good faith, the Marquess could not stop feeling elated by the idea of having the mountain of debt removed — for a time anyway.

"You own extensive property," said Mr. Barrington, returning the miniature to his pocket. "Have you never considered selling any of it?"

"No," said the Marquess harshly. "I would kill myself first."

"Ah, well, with me to take care of you, there is no need for that, no need for that at all."

Mr. Barrington got down to business and the Marquess cheerfully signed everything put in front of him. He would buy a diamond pendant for Lucy. They were going to the Ruthford's ball that very evening. Habard had said he would not be present so there was no need to be overattentive to Lucy.

On the other hand, he would not like her to find out that the vast amount of money her parents had paid him in order that he would marry her had already been dissipated.

To do the Marquess of Standish justice, he was firmly convinced that Lucy knew of the deal, knew that her parents had in effect bought him for her. It was one of the reasons he felt he did not have to always be with her, although at heart he was fonder of her than most people in his self-centered life.

His business being settled, he made a brisk farewell to Mr. Barrington and a tender one to Harriet and took himself off to Asprey's in Bond Street to find a present for his wife.

After some deliberation, he chose a diamond pendant on a delicate gold chain and diamond earrings to match.

Feeling virtuous, he arrived home in triumph and dropped the box in Lucy's lap.

To his surprise, she did not scream with delight on seeing the expensive baubles, but sat very still, turning them over slowly in her small hand.

"I-I made a list of the bills in your desk, Guy," she faltered.

"That is not your business," he said, still too surprised at her reaction to be angry. "Try them on, Lucy."

"But . . . but . . . the bills amount to fifty thousand pounds, Guy. All of them *unpaid*. And . . . and . . . I became worried because you are always saying we must retrench. And, oh! it is wonderful of you to think of me, but . . ."

"Silly, puss," teased the Marquess, trying to

fight down his rising rage. What had come over
the girl? She was normally so sweet and acqui-
escent. The buying of the baubles, he had
hoped, would give his guilty conscience over
his marital infidelity a sort of immediate abso-
lution.

"My man of business is dealing with them
right away," he said.

"Mr. Stockwell is dealing with it *all?*"

"Not Stockwell . . . that preaching old Meth-
odist. A new fellow, Barrington."

"Oh, *Guy.* That is the man I was warned
against. It is said . . ."

"A pox on what was said!" howled the Marquess, snatching the jewels and cramming them
back in the box. "The fact is you are childish
and ungrateful and do not deserve *anything.*"

"But, *listen* to me," cried Lucy, jumping to
her feet.

"No, I'll go and listen to someone who will
appreciate me."

"Harriet Comfort, no doubt."

"Why not?" he sneered. "She knows how to
make a man feel like a man!"

"Quite an achievement," flashed Lucy,
"when he does not know how to behave like
one!"

The Marquess slapped her as hard as he
could and Lucy went flying while he stormed
from the room.

The slap had been so unexpected that Lucy
had not resisted it in any way and so it did less

damage than it might.

She picked herself off the floor and found to her surprise that she no longer had any desire to cry. She was too furious for that. Furious and worried.

Something must be done to bring her husband to his senses. She was rubbing her stinging cheek when Mrs. Hartford was announced.

Ann was worried. She had heard many reports of Lucy's outing with the Duke of Habard, of how happy the Duke had appeared in Lucy's company and various descriptions of what a handsome couple they had made.

Ann was regretting her remark that Lucy should find a lover. She was worried her young friend might have taken her suggestion seriously. She felt she had joined the ranks of those dreadful women who make it their business to interfere in other couples' marriages.

Never had Lucy found herself so out of charity with her best friend. Ann burst out with, "I saw Guy crossing the square just as I was arriving. He really is a fine figure of a man, Lucy. Where *does* he get his coats made? Weston?"

"Schultz," said Lucy dully.

"Indeed? I would have said Weston. You have rather too much slap on one side of your face, my dear," added Ann innocently, not realizing that in using the cant word for rouge, she had described the source of Lucy's one-sided blush accurately.

"Have you heard of a bill broker called Barrington?" asked Lucy abruptly.

"A bill broker? No. Are you in dun territory?"

"I believe so," said Lucy, suddenly longing to tell Ann about the gift of the necklace and how it had been taken back. To stop herself from being disloyal to her husband, Lucy went on, "Probably I am making too much of it and becoming quite exercised to no good effect. Guy deals with all our business matters and naturally men know better than us women how to handle such things," added Lucy, trying to believe this to be true.

"Are you going to the Ruthfords' ball tonight?" asked Ann.

"Yes. It is to be a masked ball, you know. I have such a pretty mask, although it was vastly expensive." Once again Lucy was assailed by guilt. How *could* she be alarmed at her husband's extravagance when the things she ordered for herself were often very costly. But there must be some action she could take . . . oh, she wished Ann would go away so that she could *think*.

While her mind twisted and turned, she answered Ann's questions about Blackheath in a half-hearted kind of way which reassured that lady immediately. The Duke of Habard had broken many hearts in his time, but never had it been said that his own had been in the slightest touched.

58

Ann went on to describe the latest terrible road accident. The Honorable Mr. Butler and his sister, the Marchioness Mariescotti, had been returning from Ascot races in Mr. Butler's phaeton. He had been driving four blood horses of different colors at great speed from Englefield Green down Egham Hill, when traces, collars, and breeches had broken away and the phaeton was overturned with such force that it had *shivered* to pieces.

The leaders were killed and Mr. Butler had been pulled from his seat and dragged along the ground. The Marchioness's arm had been broken in two places and two London surgeons had been called upon to attend her and her situation was still uncertain.

And Lucy murmured shocked remarks, her mind still racing.

At last Ann took her leave and Lucy was left in peace to search for a solution to salvage the wreck of her marriage.

But try as she would, she could not think of any ideas. She did not think for a moment that the Duke had been mistaken about Mr. Barrington. He was too much a man of the world for that.

She was still turning the problem over in her mind when her parents were announced.

Mr. and Mrs. Hyde-Benton were disappointed to find the Marquess from home, but were determined that Lucy should make up for his absence by describing all the Notables she had met so that they might join the ranks of the aristocracy by proxy, as it were.

Mr. Hyde-Benton was tall and sallow with a long lugubrious face. Mrs. Hyde-Benton was fair and faded, showing some traces of earlier beauty lurking in a weak, rather silly face.

Lucy obliged them as best she could, but somehow could not bring herself to describe her day at Blackheath. Her parents, she knew, would immediately demand an exhausting and exhaustive description of everything the Duke had said and done.

Instead Lucy found herself asking, "Do you know of a Mr. Barrington who is a bill broker, Papa?"

"I have no dealings with him, but I have heard of him. Why?"

"Someone was talking about him. He has an office somewhere in the City, I believe?"

"Six Fetter Lane," said her father promptly. "But bill brokers are not fashionable. Have you seen the Prince Regent this Season?"

"I saw him briefly at the Courtlands' ball," said Lucy. Suddenly an idea of how to win back her husband's love came to her in a blinding flash. "I think we are going to a reception at the Queen's House."

"Oooh!" exclaimed Mrs. Hyde-Benton. " 'Tis montrous exciting. You will need a court dress and a hoop and . . ."

"Exactly," said Lucy firmly. "I do not wish to ask Guy for the money because men do not understand the excessive cost of these things."

"Do not worry, my love," said her mother. "Papa will gladly fund you. And . . . and . . . you must have your portrait painted. The Queen's House. Oh, dear! I shall die of excitement."

"How much?" asked Mr. Hyde-Benton.

Lucy took a deep breath. "Fifty thousand pounds," she said.

"Fifty thou—" gasped Mr. Hyde-Benton. He had thought that nothing more in the way of inflationary Regency prices could shock him. But this!

"Lady Londonderry paid a deal more," said Lucy, her heart thumping against her ribs. "You see, Papa, one's gown must be embroidered in precious stones and it is the thing to have the heels of one's shoes encrusted with diamonds. But it *is* excessive. I am flying too high."

Mr. Hyde-Benton took a deep breath. He could well afford even this vast sum of money. His daughter's social success meant everything to him.

Lucy watched him anxiously. She had no fear of her parents arriving on the supposed night of the royal reception in order to see her finery. The Hyde-Bentons were so obsessed with social climbing that they thought very little of their own status and were always careful to call on their daughter when they were sure she would not be entertaining any of her grand

61

friends. Lucy's success was enough for them. Every time her name appeared in the court circular, they cut it out and carefully pasted it into a gold-embossed book.

"Very well," said her father. "I will give you a draft on my bank. Perhaps I should give it to Lord Standish. . . ."

"Oh, but he wouldn't understand," said Lucy quickly. "And he would be shocked at the extravagance. Confess, Papa. You are shocked yourself."

"Very well," said Mr. Hyde-Benton again. "Now, Lucy, did the Prince Regent speak to you? What was he wearing? And is it true that . . . ?"

To Lucy, with the draft on her father's bank firmly in her hand, it seemed only fair to please her indulgent parents as best she could, and so, with only a little twinge of guilt, she invented a long and fictitious conversation with the Prince Regent, and, after some time, her parents left, feeling quite dizzy and exalted at the thought of their little Lucy sitting talking to His Royal Highness for quite half an hour.

The Duke of Habard waited patiently in the traffic jamming Fleet Street. Not for him the impatience of the flogging whip or loud oath.

Sooner or later, the press of carriages and brewers' drays would start to move. He found himself thinking of Lady Standish. She came so suddenly and vividly to his mind that he half turned his head, expecting to see her.

The slight form of a heavily veiled woman was turning into Fetter Lane. There was something in the walk . . . in the turn of the head . . .

The Duke frowned. The figure scurried quickly along and then turned into the dark court which led to the offices of Mr. Barrington.

The traffic began to move, and, almost against his will, he swung off Fleet Street, into Fetter Lane and the court that led to Number Six. His gaze ranged over the handful of unsavory characters who were lounging about and he was glad he had brought Harry, the burliest of his grooms, along instead of his small tiger. He did not fear for himself but for the welfare of his horses.

But he found himself reluctant to climb down and ascend the stairs to Mr. Barrington's office. He had been thinking so intensely of Lady Standish that surely it followed that he imagined the veiled woman to be she. Then if it did turn out to be Lady Standish, surely it was entirely her own affair whether she wished to apply to Barrington for help. But such a lamb in the clutches of such a wolf! Then again, whatever she did was her husband's affair, not his. At last, he came to the conclusion that unless he found out what exactly was going on in that office upstairs, he would not be able to enjoy the rest of the day.

The staircase leading to Mr. Barrington's office was dark and dirty and smelled abominably. Near the top were two burly individuals, leaning on either side of the wall.

The Duke tossed the nearest one a guinea and said in a low voice, "Be off with you and drink my health. I have private business with Mr. Barrington."

The fellow hesitated and looked at his companion, who shrugged. They were paid sixpence an hour to "defend" Mr. Barrington, but so far there had been no cause for their services. And there was only a slip of a girl in with the old man. The man with the guinea winked. "We'll just step out for a minute, guv," he muttered, and, jerking his head to his friend to follow him, he ambled off down the stairs.

The Duke waited until they had gone and then moved silently up to the door. Voices came faintly from within but he could not make out what they were saying.

He turned the handle very gently and gave the door a little push, hoping it would not creak.

Now Lucy's voice came clearly to his ears. "I do not understand, Mr. Barrington," she was saying. "I have here fifty thousand pounds in order to pay those bills of my husband's. None of them is yet overdue and yet you dare to demand some extortionate amount of interest."

"Your husband was well aware of the arrangement," replied Mr. Barrington, sounding highly amused. "He signed these papers, agreeing to the stipulated amount of discount."

"My lord is careless," said Lucy, "and I do not believe for a moment that he knew what he was signing. I will take you to court."

"I do not believe that," came Mr. Barrington's voice. The amusement had gone and he sounded irritated. "The court would uphold my claim."

"But it would expose your sharp practices to the eyes of the newspapers and public," said Lucy. For a moment the Duke could hardly believe this was the porcelain-miniature Lady Standish.

There came the sound of a chair shifting. "Look here, my little lady," said Mr. Barrington and his voice was no longer jovial but tinged with menace. "You are threatening me and I don't like threats. I see you are veiled and I should guess that you came here unattended. It would be a pity if anything should happen to the delightful Marchioness of Standish . . ."

The Duke of Habard pushed open the door.

Mr. Barrington paused in midsentence, his mouth open. Lucy swung around. She was seated in a high-backed chair facing Mr. Barrington across the desk.

The Duke raised his quizzing glass and studied the tableau.

"My Lord Duke!" gasped Mr. Barrington, who made it his job to recognize all the members of the Quality. "We have just completed our business and Lady Standish is just leaving." Mr. Barrington began to rub his thick hands. The Duke of Habard was a big fish and he was anxious to speed this irritating little Marchioness on her way.

"We have not completed our business," said Lucy in a hard clear voicc. "I have here fifty thousand pounds and I wish my husband's bills back and all the papers he signed."

"These gorgeous ladies," sighed Mr. Barrington with mock jollity. "They should not addle their pretty heads with business matters. . . ."

"Know your place, my good man," snapped Lucy, "and do not dare to patronize me!"

She returned Mr. Barrington's glare, although she was suffering from feelings of shock and dismay that the Duke, the very man who had warned her against Barrington, should turn out to be one of his clients.

"I will be with you directly, Your Grace," said Mr. Barrington.

At the Duke's reply, Lucy took a deep breath of relief.

For the Duke smiled pleasantly and said, "I have no business with such as you, Barrington, nor am I like to have. I am waiting to escort Lady Standish home."

Mr. Barrington picked up a handbell on his desk and rang it furiously.

"If you are ringing that thing to summon your yahoos, you will find them gone to the nearest tavern," said the Duke, moving forward.

"Give Lady Standish *all* the papers she requires, Barrington, and do it now, if you please."

Lucy glanced up quickly at the Duke's face. He had not raised his voice but somehow his tall figure seemed to emanate cold anger.

For a long moment Mr. Barrington and the Duke stood looking at each other.

Mr. Barrington rapidly came to a decision that it would be politic to give Lady Standish what she wanted. But somehow he would ruin the Standishes, somehow he would get the Marquess back into his clutches.

"Very well, Your Grace," he said mildly. He lumbered off into an adjoining room where he could be heard shuffling through files and papers.

Lucy clenched her hands into fists in her lap to hide their sudden trembling. She glanced up at the Duke's stern profile and he turned and looked down, immediately aware of her gaze. His lips curved in a smile and one eyelid drooped in a mocking wink.

It all seemed like a dream to Lucy. In no time at all, she found herself perched up beside the Duke on his phaeton, clutching a sheaf of bills and papers and breathing in deep gulps of sooty London air.

The Duke had dismissed his groom. Lucy waited rather apprehensively for the lecture

67

that she was sure he was about to deliver. But he merely said pleasantly, "It is a wonderful day. If you are not too anxious to return home immediately, we may drive to the Park and enjoy the air."

Lucy nodded shyly. The Duke proceeded to enliven the short journey by entertaining Lucy with stories of the Lady Jehus who made driving in the London streets a risky adventure. There was Lady Archer, for example, who was the terror of the West End from the pace at which she drove; then there was Lady Stewart with her famous four grays; and a Mrs. Garden from Portland Street who won a considerable bet by driving her phaeton and bays from Grosvenor Gate through the Park to Kensington in five and a half minutes.

On reaching the Park, he pointed out the Prince Regent, driving with St. Leger in a carriage and pair, with blue harness edged with red, the horses' manes decorated with scarlet ribbons and the Prince's plumes on their crests, the carriage itself lined with rose-colored satin and festoons of rich gold braid.

Then there was Lord Rodney, driving his nag-tailed horses, and Lord Petersham driving his brown carriage and brown horses and dressed from head to foot in brown and all for the love of a Mrs. Brown, and Mr. Tommy Onslow, the T.O. of the cartoonists, and Mr. Charles Finch wearing a servant's livery. And . . .

The Duke broke off for a second and then

said, "These carriages kick up so much dust. Let us find a quieter part of the Park."

To his relief, Lucy agreed without demur and he was able to swing his phaeton round and away from the fascinating spectacle presented by a very tipsy Marquess of Standish, driving Harriet Comfort, before his fair companion managed to see it.

The Duke drove at a very slow pace until they were away from the fashionable crowd and then reined in his horses.

"You must be wondering what I was doing in Mr. Barrington's office," began Lucy.

"No," he said quietly. "What you were doing was easily understandable. But I do feel compelled to offer you a word of advice."

"Which is?" asked Lucy nervously.

"It is this. You cannot prevent your husband from the consequences of his folly forever."

"But he will be so relieved, so overjoyed to find I have taken the load of debt from his shoulders that he will . . . will be more prudent in future."

Poor thing, poor silly little thing, thought the Duke angrily. She was about to say, "so that he will take me in his arms and say he loves me."

"It is very hard to be prudent when one is a hardened gamester," he said. "London abounds in hells, all capable of taking the estates away from the best families in England. There's the House with the Red Baize Door in Bennet Street, the Pigeon Hole at Ten St. James's

Square, Mrs. Leache's and Mr. Davis's in King Street, and hundreds of others. I have witnessed the frenzy of the losers. I have seen proud men, weeping like statues without moving a muscle of their faces, and with nothing to show they were alive but the tears running down their cheeks.

"There is a record of a ruined man seizing the edge of the table in his teeth and dying in the act. The company fled horrified and he was found by the watch, dead, with his eyes open, his face distorted, and his teeth driven far into the wood of the table. A Frenchman was seen to ram a billiard ball down his throat, whence it was removed by a surgeon; an Irishman put a lighted candle into his mouth. A gamester, whose nonchalance at repeated losses was remarked upon, opened his shirt and showed his chest all lacerated by his own fingernails.

"My dear Lady Standish, your only solution is to persuade your husband to return to the country. He is very young, not much older than yourself, I believe."

"But . . . but it is not fashionable in the country," said Lucy weakly.

"No," he agreed with an edge to his voice. "There are all those unfashionable tenants who rely on us for a livelihood and decent housing. If our estates go on the gambling table, what becomes of them?"

"I will try," said Lucy like a patient child responding to the severe lecturing of a stern parent.

He turned and looked at her in sudden compassion. He wanted to tell her that he would do everything in the world to help her be happy. And then he remembered that Lady Standish was married and that her marital troubles were none of his business. His mind clamped down on these strange new emotions, and he gently set his horses in motion.

"How solemn we have become!" he said lightly. "I gather you are to attend the Ruthfords' masked ball tonight?"

"Yes," said Lucy, "but you, Your Grace, have other plans?"

"Perhaps I might change them," he found himself saying, much to his irritation. This friendship with Lucy Standish must cease. He was becoming too . . . interested.

It was late afternoon and long shafts of golden sunlight were slanting through the translucent spring green of the trees.

The air was warm with a hint of summer. Lucy found herself wishing she would never reach home — home with all its agonies of lost love and rejection. It would be pleasant to drive on forever beside this austere companion, on out into the spring countryside far from the dirt and glitter of the city.

But when he lifted her down from the carriage, after having called on one of the Standish footmen to hold the horses, and she felt his hands at her waist and saw those strange silver eyes holding her own, felt the trembling of her legs and the way her treacherous body seemed to be melting towards him, she became aware of a sense of danger, aware that any journey with the enigmatic Duke might not end in the tranquil way it had begun.

She could not analyze, could not understand the effect his very lightest and most impersonal touch had on her whole body. Gathering her wits, she entered the house to be told that the Marquess of Standish was at home. Lucy was quite confident that the Duke would shortly be proved wrong. Men thought they understood men — but surely no one understood a man better than his own wife.

The subsequent row was of such a magnitude that even the prophetic Duke of Habard would have been startled.

It was as well that Lucy forebore from explaining that the Duke of Habard had been witness to the business transaction. It was as well the Marquess had not seen her with the Duke in the Park. He considered she had disgraced him enough.

She had behaved in a grossly unfeminine way, he railed. He had had a good run at the tables and would have shortly come about. Barrington was a sterling fellow. All the Fashionables went to Barrington. Damme, if the story got about, he would have to leave Town.

And that was when poor Lucy suggested

leaving Town might be a very good idea indeed.

And that was when the Marquess told her that he should have known better than to marry a country bumpkin with straw for a brain. She was a yokel, insipid, a disgrace to any man of breeding. He *hated* her with all his heart and soul!

"There are other men who find me attractive," shouted Lucy, quite overwrought.

"Oh, no doubt some Cit or mushroom fascinated by your title," he sneered. "No man of the ton would give you a second glance."

"And *you* consider it a mark of good breeding to consort with poxy harlots like Harriet Comfort," said Lucy, suddenly as cold as she had been hot with fury a moment before.

The Marquess drew himself up to his full height. "Harriet Comfort is fashionable," he said awfully. "You, madame, are not."

"Oh, Guy," sighed Lucy. "Do, please do stop making such a cake of yourself."

"I shall go where I am wanted," said the Marquess, retreating, stiff-legged, like a hound before a formidable adversary.

"I'm sure every card-sharp and ivory turner and lightskirt in Seven Dials will give you a resounding welcome," said Lucy sweetly.

The banging of the drawing room door was his lordship's answer to that.

For a few moments, Lucy felt exultant. The

worm had turned. She had told him what she thought of him. But then she was overwhelmed by a great engulfing wave of despair for lost love.

But this time, she did not cry.

Chapter Four

At least Lucy did not wait until the last minute, hoping her husband would join her. She was grateful for the pretty gold mask which hid most of her face. Her hair was intricately twisted up on top of her head and threaded with topazes on thin gold chains. A heavy topaz and gold necklace was around her neck and her tunic dress of white silk was ornamented with a gold key pattern.

The ballroom was crowded. No one — not even Ann — now troubled to ask the whereabouts of the Marquess. But the gossips were busy. Most of the guests had been informed of the Marquess's appearance in the Park with Harriet Comfort and of how the Duke of Habard had driven Lady Standish away from that shameful sight. Lucy received many looks of pity and began to feel irritated since she did not know the cause. She assumed they were sorry for her because she had had to arrive alone. But then so did quite a number of married ladies — well, one or two. She put on a commendable show of a young matron without a care in the world.

Lady Londonderry was there, wearing so many jewels that she had to be followed around by her footman carrying a chair since her ladyship could only take a few steps at a time, burdened as she was by the glittering weight of diamonds and rubies and pearls.

The Dandies were very much in evidence, polishing their wit at someone else's expense as usual and talking in their convoluted Tom and Jerry cant.

People came and went. Unlike Lucy, most of the Fashionables prided themselves on accepting at least twenty-four invitations a day and they usually could only manage to honor each occasion with ten minutes of their presence.

Although it was a masked ball, it was not a fancy-dress affair and most people were immediately recognizable. At midnight, there was a general unmasking with everyone exclaiming in surprise as if they were not very well aware of who their partner was.

It was after supper, somewhere around 1:30 in the morning, when most of the Fashionables had returned from their other engagements and when there was a lull in the dancing that the Marquess of Standish made his appearance. He had a female on his arm. Both were masked.

Lucy turned quite white. For the lady on her husband's arm was wearing diamond earrings and a diamond pendant, the same that her husband had tried to give to her and then had taken back.

The Duke of Ruthfords moved forward to greet the late guests. He had a high penetrating voice.

"Ah, Standish!" he cried. "You are come too late. The unmasking was at midnight, so you see you must unveil."

The Marquess murmured something. He staggered slightly showing he was in his usual tipsy state.

"No! No!" cried the Duke. "You shall not take away this fair charmer."

"Unmask!" cried the other guests, crowding into a circle around the Marquess and his companion. Lucy was jostled and shoved to the front of the circle.

Behind the slits of his mask, the Marquess's eyes held a hunted look, as if he had suddenly sobered up and found himself in the middle of a nightmare.

At least it's not Harriet Comfort, thought Lucy. This woman has red hair.

The Marquess hesitated, looking this way and that.

"Why not?" laughed his companion. She lifted her hands and untied the strings of her mask.

"No," said the Marquess hoarsely.

"Come along, Standish," laughed the Duke of Ruthfords. "We all know it's you."

The lady let her mask drop to her side and stood facing them defiantly, the other hand fingering the diamond pendant at her throat.

It was Harriet Comfort in a red wig.

There was a shocked murmur. Standish had gone too far this time. He had brought London's leading Cyprian to one of London's most exclusive balls.

"Outrageous!" fumed the Duke, stalking off. The circle of guests began to melt away, talking in shocked, hushed whispers. The Duke of Ruthfords could be heard calling angrily for music. The opening strains of a waltz struck up.

Harriet looked at Lucy with a mocking glint in her eyes. The Marquess flushed miserably and shuffled his feet. Lucy took a step towards them, her hands balled into fists.

"No, I think not, Lady Standish!"

A tall figure blocked her view of her husband and his mistress. The Duke of Habard's cool gray eyes held Lucy's burning ones.

"My dance, I think, Lady Standish," he said. One strong arm circled her waist and bore her off into the steps of the waltz.

"Try to look as if nothing had happened," said the Duke's voice in her ear.

"I c-can't," said Lucy, her voice breaking on a sob. "I-I'm going to cry."

"And let that trollop see your distress? They are leaving. Ruthfords has ordered them out and quite right too. No, don't look!"

"It's n-no use," said Lucy pathetically. "I *am* going to cry."

The Duke of Habard twirled her expertly straight across the floor until they were at the long, open french windows which led out into the garden.

Holding her arm in a firm clasp, he urged her down the shallow steps which led to the lawn.

"*Now* you may cry," he said pleasantly.

But Lucy found she did not want to cry anymore. The cool dark air of the garden closed around her as he led her across the grass, away from the jaunty mocking music of the ballroom.

"Why did you come?" she asked. "You said you would not come."

"My other engagement seemed flat. I was going home and saw Standish alighting with Miss Comfort on his arm."

"How did you know it was she? *I* did not know until she unmasked. She was wearing a red wig."

"Her figure was familiar," he said dryly.

"And you came to help me? Oh, thank you," said Lucy in a muffled voice. "You always seem to be helping me."

"And I must stop. You are old enough to handle your own marriage, Lady Standish."

He pulled out a pocket handkerchief and dusted the seat of a marble bench which glimmered palely in the moonlight at the far end of the garden.

"Sit down, Lady Standish," he said. "I will stay with you until you are quite recovered and then I will take you home."

Lucy sat down and stared at the grass at her feet. She was consumed with a desire for revenge. She wanted to hurt her fickle husband as much as he had hurt her. How would he like it if she paraded her infatuation for a man before the eyes of society?

And then, clear as a bell, Ann Hartford's teasing voice urging her to take a lover sounded in her brain.

She turned and looked at the Duke of Habard. He had lit a thin black cheroot and seemed totally absorbed in blowing smoke rings up to the starry sky. The cry of the watch calling two o'clock came faintly to Lucy's ears.

Why not? Why not ask this fashionable Duke to be her inamorato? Had she not been so over-wrought, Lucy would never have considered for a moment asking such a paragon to be her lover.

But hurt and a thirst for revenge had driven away Lady Lucy's customary timidity.

All at once she said, "My Lord Duke, I wish to ask you a very great favor."

"Ask away," said the Duke easily. "Although I cannot guarantee that I will be able to help you."

"I wish you to be my lover," said Lucy.

He sat very still, and then he very carefully extinguished his cheroot, turned on the seat, and looked down at her. He was about to say something along the lines of how dare she use him thus to revenge herself on her useless husband. But her hair glimmered in the moonlight like pale gold and her shoulders rising above the low neckline of her gown were very white. She smelled faintly of flowers and powder. He sighed a little. She was not serious. Only hurt. He would frighten her out of the idea without humiliating her.

"Very well," he said lazily. "My servants are very discreet. You may come home with me, or, if you would prefer it, we can find some inn a little out of town and there we may consummate this burning passion which obviously consumes you."

"No!" exclaimed Lucy. "I mean, that is not the way it should be."

"Ah, you must instruct me. I am not in the way of having liaisons with respectable married ladies."

"Well . . . well . . . we should flirt a little and . . . and . . . get to know one another first."

"How dull!"

"Oh, Your Grace, you are mocking me. And you are *very* kind. You know I only asked you because I want revenge on Guy."

"Yes," he agreed amiably. "I find it rather refreshing. I am so used to ladies throwing themselves at my title and fortune that I had quite begun to think myself irresistible. You are very good for me, Lady Lucy, rather like rhubarb pills or cold baths or —"

"I'm sorry," interrupted Lucy in a small voice.

"There. I will not tease you anymore. I shall pretend to be your lover for a little while, but do not be surprised if that husband of yours calls me out."

"Oh, Guy would never do a thing like that. Do you think he will be jealous . . . just a little?"

"I think he will be very jealous. But you must play your part. *You* must appear to be in love with me."

"I th-think I could manage that," said Lucy, her voice breaking on a sob.

"Not if you are going to go around looking sad and haunted. Take my hands and hold them firmly. Look up at me! Good. Now. Pretend you are wildly, madly, and passionately in love with me."

Lucy looked up into his face. His eyes glittered strangely in the moonlight and she could feel the hard pressure of his hands.

"No. You looked scared and lost," he said. "You need encouragement. One of your curls has come loose."

He took off his gloves and gently lifted a long curl from her shoulder, letting his fingertips linger for a moment on her skin. Then he gently wound it back into place among the others pinned on top of her head.

"You must call me Simon," he said caressingly, stroking her cheek with the back of his hand, "and I shall call you Lucy.

"Listen! Someone is coming. Ah, if I am not mistaken, that high chattering voice belongs to one of London's worst gossips, Mrs. Partington. She has commandeered some gentleman to show her the flowers but she really wants to find out what we are doing. So we shall not disappoint her."

Before she could guess what he was about, he had jerked her roughly into his arms and covered her mouth with his own. He pulled away a fraction and said against her lips, "Do not tremble so, dear Lucy. *Do* act your part. Mrs. Partington will do the rest." Then his mouth came down on hers again, cool and firm at first, and then burning, passionate, exploring. Lucy's body was pressed against his — she dizzily felt it was *fusing* with his — and then she felt nothing but a hectic, burning, passionate yearning. There was a shocked exclamation from Mrs. Partington and Lucy would have drawn away, but the Duke held her very tightly while Mrs. Partington's companion muttered, "By Jove, I think that's Habard," and then Lucy heard the sound of hurriedly retreating footsteps.

The Duke had meant to release her as soon as the inquisitive Mrs. Partington had seen enough, but his senses were taking over completely from his brain, and the inside of her mouth tasted sweet to his exploring tongue, and her breasts were pressed so hard against him, and . . .

He jerked away roughly and said in a rather ragged voice, "I think we performed our parts rather well. That wretched curl has escaped from its mooring again and you look quite wanton. See, I shall pin it back with its fellows."

His voice sounded normal again. "Shall we join the curious gossips in the ballroom? Have you eaten?"

"I tried to at supper, but I could not."

"Then we shall both eat," said the Duke lightly.

He helped Lucy to her feet and she took his arm. They moved slowly like sleepwalkers across the grass, each of them stunned with the violence of their feelings.

When they were both seated in the supper room, each studied the other with veiled curiosity.

She looks so fragile and virginal, thought the Duke in surprise. And yet his emotions have never been so overset before. Perhaps it was the atmosphere of the garden. She looks so *pure* sitting there, little more than a schoolgirl.

He looks as cold and formal as usual, Lucy was thinking. What *can* he be thinking of me. I have never responded like that, even to Guy. It must have been because my nerves were so overset.

To Ann Hartford, standing at the door of the supper room, they seemed entirely insulated from their surroundings by their interest in each other. She took a half-step forward, and then stopped.

"What is the matter?" asked Giles Hartford. "I thought we were to take Lucy home."

"She is with Habard," said Ann bleakly. "Oh, what have I done?"

"Done! Done?" Giles peered over his wife's thin shoulder but did not see what she saw. Lucy and the Duke of Habard looked, to him, totally uninterested in one another.

"You have done nothing," said Giles Hartford. "If Standish chooses to disgrace himself, it is nothing to do with you."

"But I said — you know, just as a joke — that Lucy should take a lover just to bring that husband of hers to his senses."

"Well, if you mean Habard, you are very much mistaken. He's hardly led the life of a monk, but on the other hand he has never shown a *tendre* for married women of any kind. You are overtired, my dear, and overworried on behalf of your friend. Let us go home ourselves. You may see Lucy tomorrow and offer her the comfort she needs. We are quite safe to leave her with Habard."

The Marquess of Standish clutched his head. Harriet Comfort leaned indolently against the blue silk upholstery of her carriage and looked at him with something approaching hate.

Earlier that day she had received a note from Mr. Barrington promising her a large sum of money should she manage to ruin Standish.

She had shrugged and thrown it away, for of all her beaux, she rather liked the handsome Marquess. But he had gone too far. As they had left the ball, he had bemoaned the social ruin he had brought upon himself by taking "a harlot" into society.

The Marquess was too distressed and too tipsy to know what he was saying, but his words had cut deep. Harriet Comfort craved respectability and was, most of the time, able to ignore the fact that she was not *comme il faut,* soothed and flattered and courted as she was by the most eminent gentlemen of society. Now she wanted revenge on the Marquess and revenge on that silly milkmaid wife of his who had looked at her with such disgust and horror.

"Guy, Guy," she cooed soothingly. "What a great fuss you are making. You forget who I am. You forget that most men at that ball would give their right arm to spend one night with me. Why! Tomorrow you will be the admiration of the clubs."

The Marquess looked at her blearily. "Do . . . do you think so, Harriet?"

"I know so. Have I ever been wrong in matters of fashion? Now I am going to take you someplace quite exotic. Have you ever seen a Chinese woman?"

The Marquess shook his head.

"Then relax, and I shall provide you with such a night of pleasure that you will forget all else."

The carriage had been traveling for some time and came to a stop outside a huddle of tall buildings.

"Where are we?" asked the Marquess.

"Somewhere near the river," Harriet smiled. "Come."

The Marquess followed her from the carriage, shivering as the chill of the night air and the raw damp smell of the river struck him.

Harriet knocked at a low door and waited until the judas was opened. A face stared at her and then the door was unlocked.

The Marquess found himself in a low, lamplit room. There were two mattresses on the floor. And at the far end of the room, a Chinese woman was half lying on a sofa.

He drew in his breath in an alarmed hiss, wondering at first if he were seeing some fantastic statue.

"Her name is Li," murmured Harriet's voice at his ear.

She was very small. Her face was a delicate mask of paint and jewels. A heavy jeweled headdress concealed all of her hair. Her eyebrows were two brush strokes. Her embroidered gown shimmered and winked in the lamplight and her fingers with long, long nails seemed too fragile to hold the weight of glittering rings. Her tiny bound feet in their white stockings just peeped below the hem of her fantastic costume. Only the eyes were alive, almond-shaped, burning, watching.

Two Chinese men came quietly into the room and set about placing a little tray of tools, pipes, a lamp, and a glass jar on a lacquered table they had carried in with them.

"We sit down here," said Harriet, indicating one of the mattresses. "What do you think of Li?"

"Terrible. Monstrous," breathed the Marquess. The almond eyes blazed like topazes in the light of a fire and then died down to a gold shimmer.

"Does she understand English?" asked the Marquess nervously.

"I do not know," said Harriet indifferently. "I have never known her to speak."

"And does she . . . will she . . . ?"

"Only for a great price."

"But what Englishman would . . . ?"

"Shhh!" admonished Harriet.

One of the Chinese men stooped over the Marquess and offered him a small pipe.

"What is this?" snapped the Marquess, who was sobering rapidly. "This mummery has gone on long enough. Let us go?"

"After you smoke," said Harriet, smiling into his eyes. "It is the custom of the house."

"And *then* can I go?" asked the Marquess like a petulant child.

"Then you can go."

The Marquess took the thin jade pipe in his fingers and drew in the smoke.

Gradually the room shimmered and drifted and faded and he was wandering in a dream country of green and gold. He had never known such release from care, such happiness.

By the time dawn spread over London he had

smoked six pipes, had dreamily signed his name to the bills required without noticing the horrendous price, and had fallen under the spell of the unmoving Li. Between his opium dreams, he increasingly longed to possess her, to find out what wonders lay beneath those glittering robes.

Harriet knew he would stay for as long as she let him. But she wanted to remove him, knowing he would crave a return journey within only a few hours, knowing he would pay anything and agree to anything, only so long as she brought him back to this lamplit room by the river.

Chapter Five

For the next two weeks, the Standishes were conspicuous by their absence from society. The Marquess slept most of the day and disappeared as soon as dusk fell. He would not tell his wife where he went and Lucy did not ask. In the little time he spent with her, however, he was tender and loving and strangely apologetic. He swore he was not spending his time with Harriet Comfort, swore it with such a burning sincerity that Lucy believed him, and with that she had to be content.

For her own part, she preferred to hide at home and read. She had been appalled in retrospect by her overtures to the Duke of Habard. A young life of respectability dies hard. The new tenderness of the Marquess gave Lucy renewed hope. He had even gone so far as to thank her awkwardly for having pulled him out of debt and had apologized for striking her.

Lucy thought often of the Duke of Habard, thought often of the violent emotions his lightest touch amused in her body, and, as the sunny days passed, she decided her strange feelings must have been engendered by guilt and fear. In his absence, the Duke seemed a chilly, aloof, formidable man. And a dangerous one. What did she know of him?

To Ann Hartford, it seemed as if the Standishes' marriage was finally on a sound footing. Lucy did not tell her of Guy's nightly absences, and, when Ann called, all she saw was a loving, attentive husband. She wrongly guessed that they were having a second honeymoon, which explained the reason why Lucy had stopped to go about, and, after two calls, Ann tactfully stayed away.

Only a few months ago, Lucy would have demanded furiously to know where her husband spent his nights. But now she was frightened and lonely and prepared to grasp at any straw. If Guy's strange nightly absences meant he was becoming tender and more loving during the day, then she was gratefully prepared to accept things as they were. Her parents still eagerly demanded news of her expensive wardrobe, and reluctantly she lied.

Everything had to be sacrificed on the altar of the survival of the Standish marriage.

Harriet Comfort had sent several perfumed notes requesting the presence of the Marquess of Standish. But the Marquess no longer needed her. Every night he went down to the base of the tenement on the river to worship at the bound feet of his almond-eyed goddess, Li, to take the air in an opium trance, to dream of possessing her.

Nothing else mattered to him but this one obsession. No longer did the fashionable world exist. He was kind and considerate to his wife out of a humble gratitude that she did not question his odd comings and goings.

He hazily remembered signing a bill on the understanding that he could explore the mysteries beneath the glittering, heavy robes that very evening.

His palms were damp and his heart thumped against his ribs as he let himself quietly out of his house into the late evening light of Clarence Square. He hailed a passing hack, snarling impatiently at the Jehu and offering double the fare when the man showed signs of hesitation when he heard the address.

The fashionable squares of the West End were soon left behind, then the bustle of the Strand, then the trim streets of the City. Now the buildings became older and more dilapidated and the dank smell of the river grew stronger. The sky paled into night and occasional ragged figures could be seen scuttling like rats from doorway to doorway.

A thin mist like old yellow chiffon hung at the end of the narrow street. The tenement loomed above him, gaunt and black and strangely lifeless.

He took a deep breath, forcing himself to be calm, waiting until the curious cab driver had left the street.

Then he strode forward and knocked impatiently at the low door.

There was no reply, no oriental face appearing at the judas.

He knocked again.

Silence.

A rat scurried over his foot and he gave an exclamation of disgust, beating his hands furiously on the door.

He began to panic. Somewhere behind that unmoving door lay a magic world of opium dreams . . . somewhere sat Li, watching, ever watching, her strange topaz eyes burning in her white mask of a face.

Worked up into a mad frenzy, he smashed his broad shoulder into the door again and again, heedless of the pain.

At last he drew back, shaking and sweating, staring in anguish at the silent building.

He drew a pistol from one of the capacious pockets of his coat and primed it with trembling fingers. Then steadying his shaking hand, he took careful aim and fired at the lock.

The report sounded appallingly loud and he found himself expecting to hear the wooden rattle of the watch.

But the door swung open, revealing a black cavern, and the street remained as silent as before.

He strode in.

The black air smelled faintly of incense. He struck a lucifer and saw a stub of a candle and lit it.

The room was empty. He noticed for the first time that the floor was dirty and the walls scabrous.

93

He turned helplessly this way and that like an enraged bull.

Li and her Chinese companions had quite evidently left.

He ran out into the street, shouting, "Hey! Anybody about! Halloo!"

He sensed rather than saw that he was being watched. At the far end of the street, shadows flitted and moved in the now pitch blackness, but no one came forward or answered his calls. He hammered on various doors, and although he heard shuffling sounds within, no one came to answer.

After walking two streets distant, he came across a low tavern and pushed open the door, recoiling slightly at the stench from the dregs of humanity who were slumped about the low room.

His questions were met with brutish, sullen stares until he held out a piece of gold, repeating over and over again, "The Chinese . . . where have they gone?"

A nimble little man, a rat-catcher, with the skins of his trade hanging from his belt, detached himself from the drinkers and led the Marquess outside.

"A flash cull like ye'sel, don't wan't none o' this ken," he said, twitching the coin from the Marquess's fingers. "They Heathen 'as gone an' good riddance."

"Where?" demanded the Marquess, reaching out to seize the rat-catcher.

But the little man was too fast for him. "Gone," he cackled, skipping off down the street. "Gone!" his voice echoed in the dank air.

"Gone," he cackled from the corner of the street.

The Marquess stood with his hands clenched.

Harriet!

He let out a long sigh of relief.

Harriet was the tie. Harriet had brought him here. He had never asked her how she had come to know of such a strange place. Harriet would know where they had gone.

He had to run through street after mean street, through bewildering twists and turns until he was at last able to find a hack.

It was unfortunate that Lucy had chosen that very evening to emerge from her seclusion. Ann had lent her the first volume of a new novel and Lucy had suddenly, on impulse, decided to call on her friend to borrow the second volume. She had not stayed above half an hour. Her carriage was returning home, and, as it passed Manchester Square, Lucy glanced idly in the direction of Harriet Comfort's house.

Flambeaux were sputtering and flaring in iron brackets on the wall outside. Obviously Miss Comfort was entertaining. But it was the scene on the doorstep of the house that held Lucy's gaze, that made her rap impatiently on the roof for the coachman to stop.

Sweating, frantic, and disheveled, the Marquess of Standish was hammering on the door.

As if moving in a nightmare, Lucy opened the carriage door and climbed down.

As she approached the house, flanked by the two footmen who had been hanging on the backstrap of the carriage and who had quickly descended to escort her, Lucy felt as if she were walking in a nightmare. She wanted to cry out, "Guy!" — but was held back by the conventions, by the very presence of her servants.

As she approached, the door swung open and Harriet Comfort herself appeared on the threshold. She was wearing a circlet of diamonds in her thick brown hair, and the diamond pendant and diamond earrings that the Marquess had given her blazed at her ears and at her throat.

Lucy stood stock still.

"Harriet," she heard her husband say brokenly. "You must help me. Only you can help me."

"Silly boy," murmured Harriet, winding her arms around his neck and drawing him gently into the house. The door slammed.

Two spots of color burned on Lucy's white cheeks.

It was the ultimate, the final humiliation.

When she returned home accompanied by her wooden-faced servants, Lucy plunged into a fever of activity. She selected several gold-embossed invitations from the card rack and then hurried to her rooms, calling for her lady's maid. In no time at all she was attired in her finest robe of celestial blue chiffon. A heavy sapphire necklace was wound about her neck and sapphires were threaded through her golden hair. Carefully applied rouge had been painted on her cheeks and her eyes blazed with a hard blue glitter like her jewels.

She made her appearance at Almack's just before the doors closed at eleven. Her eyes restlessly searched the rooms. There was no sign of the Duke of Habard.

She left after only a few minutes. Her restless searching took her then to the opera, from the opera to a *musicale* at Lady Sanders's. Still no sign of the Duke.

She was about to leave the *musicale* when she saw the stocky figure of Lord Harry Brothers, who she remembered was said to be an intimate of the Duke.

She had been introduced to Lord Brothers during her first Season, and since that gentleman was lingering in the hall obviously looking for an excuse to escape, she was able to engage him in conversation and then ask as casually as she could whether the Duke was still in town.

"Oh, very much so," said Lord Brothers, looking at the pretty Lady Standish somewhat awkwardly. After all, that Partington woman had been circulating some curst odd rumors about Lady Standish and Simon, Duke of

Habard. "Seems he might be getting leg-shackled at last."

"Indeed," said Lucy, languidly fanning herself. "And who is the lucky lady, pray?"

"Oh, the Mortland chit. He has gone to some affair at their place at Kensington. I teased him about it, but you know Simon. Very close about his affairs."

Lucy changed the subject although she longed to be off. At last, Lady Brothers appeared to claim her husband and Lucy was able to slip away.

She racked her brains trying to remember whether she had received an invitation to the Mortlands' party. And in any case, if she returned home to search for it she would lose valuable time. She hesitated at the hall door and then quickly turned and threaded her way through the guests until she came to the drawing room. There were various invitations in a card rack on a small table by the fireplace.

She pretended to stumble and knocked the invitation cards flying over the carpet. Various guests stooped to help her recover them. The name Mortland seemed to leap up at her and she quickly scooped it up and managed to hide it in her reticule during all the fuss of putting the cards back in the rack.

By the time she reached the Mortlands' house, the watch was crying two o'clock. The air was chill and damp and a thin mist was winding around the trees of Kensington.

The Mortlands were never to forgive the Marchioness of Standish.

Their daughter, Charlotte, had danced *twice* at Almack's the previous Wednesday with the Duke of Habard and Mr. and Mrs. Mortland had hoped for a dazzling match. The party, although most of London society had been asked to it, was simply to supply Charlotte with an opportunity of furthering her acquaintance with the Duke.

Habard had arrived some time after midnight and the Mortlands' hopes, which had sunk to a very low ebb, had reanimated. Dancing was in progress and although the Duke had not yet asked Charlotte to partner him, it was expected he would at any moment.

And then all at once Lady Standish appeared. She walked straight up to him and said in a queer breathless voice, "I have been looking for you *everywhere*, Simon. I must speak to you."

The Duke looked down at her thoughtfully. He noticed the glittering, hectic eyes and the trembling hands.

All his intelligence told him that he should make a few polite remarks and go and dance with Miss Mortland. In fact, he almost made up his mind to do so, but at the same time he took Lucy's hand, and all the Mortlands and their guest seemed to magically disappear, leaving him alone with this little Marchioness who clung so fiercely to his hand.

So instead he said quietly, "Gently, my dear.

Do not make a scene. We will find somewhere quiet where we can talk," and, oblivious of at least one hundred pairs of eyes boring into his well-tailored back, he led her from the room.

He stood with her in the hall, irresolute, aware all at once of all the doors to the hall standing open, and of all the faces watching them curiously.

"No doubt I shall find some excuse to explain your behavior," he murmured. "Shall I take you home?"

"Not there," said Lucy urgently. "Just take me away."

He hesitated, knowing he should return and make his *adieux* to his hosts, but he felt that if he left her for a moment, she would run away.

So instead, he told a footman to have his carriage brought around and to tell Lady Standish's servants to return home without her.

He led her outside onto the step so as to escape the staring faces.

She stood shivering, clutching tightly onto his hand, until he helped her into his carriage and took his place beside her.

It was a closed carriage and she was unchaperoned, Lucy realized wildly, and then almost laughed that she should worry about conventions at this late date.

The Duke gently released her hand and leaned his head back against the upholstery. "Where shall I tell my coachman to take us?" he asked in a colorless voice.

"Anywhere," said Lucy harshly. "Preferably to your bed."

"You shock me," he said lightly.

"You . . . you *agreed* to be my lover."

"If you will remember, I agreed to *appear* as your lover."

"You do not w-want me?"

The voice in the darkness of the carriage was trembling and childish.

"You are overset," he said. "I was not surprised when I no longer saw you about. You are not the sort of lady to look for an extramarital liaison. Something has now happened to distress you."

"I should not discuss my husband."

"No. But sometimes disloyalty is necessary, especially if one wants to preserve the marriage. Forget about me as a lover and think of me as a friend. You must tell me, Lucy."

There was a long silence. And then she began, hesitantly, to tell him of Guy's strange behavior and of how he had sworn his absence at night had nothing to do with Harriet Comfort and how she had seen him, wild and distraught, on the steps of that lady's house.

He gave a little sigh. "There are three sides to every marriage, Lady Lucy," he said, "his, hers and the truth. Was he really as exercised as you say, or was he simply a trifle elated?"

"If you mean, was he drunk, the answer is no. He was wild, desperate, anguished. A man desperately in need of comfort." Lucy gave a brittle laugh. "I did not mean to pun."

He took her hand in a warm, firm clasp but she drew it away. "I feel . . . odd . . . and breathless when you touch me," she said.

She could feel his gaze on her. "Perhaps you are a trifle faint," he said, deliberately misunderstanding her. "Would you like the glasses down?"

"Yes, please, My Lord Duke."

"Simon," he corrected, lowering the window of the carriage.

Lucy gratefully took a deep breath of damp night air, smelling the wet scent of the flowers in the Kensington nurseries.

"Where do you wish me to take you?" asked the Duke again.

"Home with you."

"Ah, that I could. I have such a reputation and yet I am plagued with respectability. I have a trifle of vanity too which makes me balk at being . . . er . . . used. Your husband is young and wild and not yet used to the responsibilities of marriage. *Ask* him the reason for his behavior."

"I am afraid."

"Of what?"

"Of the final rejection. Of his telling me that he loves Harriet Comfort to distraction. Many women in society ignore such liaisons . . . are *expected* to ignore them. I would like to see . . . to see if I could make him a little jealous. It is not a worthy ambition, but a very human one. I should not burden you with my troubles. Your friend Lord Brothers believed you to be on the point of becoming affianced to Miss Mortland."

"Alas, no."

Lucy began to feel quite lighthearted but could not understand why. "But you will no doubt wish to become married?" she said.

"No."

"Why?"

"Why not? You are not precisely a good advertisement for wedded bliss."

"Cruel."

"But true."

"Then you do not wish to be my lover?"

"My dear Lady Lucy, any man with all his faculties and his wits would be delighted to be your lover. I am sorely tempted to tell you to find someone else but I fear all are not as scrupulous as myself. There are, however, certain young gentlemen of a certain effeminacy who would be glad to play the role of sighing lover."

"They would not make Guy jealous."

"And I would? Dear me, how stubborn you are. What if my passions should overcome me?"

Lucy looked at him, at the calm profile revealed by the bobbing light of the carriage lamps, and said with a trace of humor in her voice, "I cannot imagine you being carried away by passion."

"Do not be too sure of that. But before we decide to do anything, I entreat you to return home and, if your husband is there, I beg you to question him."

"Very well," sighed Lucy.

"I think you will find him very contrite. These young bloods are lions at night and meek little lambs in the morning. I remember the follies of my own youth."

"You talk as if you are old."

"I am . . . compared to you."

They jogged on in silence until Clarence Square was reached. He helped her from the carriage and stood looking down at her.

"Do you know, Lucy," he said softly, "I think this is the very last I shall hear of this idea." He glanced up at the house. "There is a light still burning abovestairs. No doubt it is your husband. Go to his arms where you belong and cease to tantalize hardened *roués* such as myself."

"You find me very young and silly."

He looked at her seriously for a long moment and then raised her hand to his lips.

"On the contrary, I find you *adorable*," he said.

Lucy felt an overwhelming urge to throw herself into his arms, to bury her head in his chest, to beg him to take her away.

But her conscience, clear and strong, told her where her duty lay. She caught up her long skirts and ran lightly up the stairs.

As she put her hand on the knob, something impelled her to turn and look at him.

He was standing beside the carriage, regarding her gravely. A light breeze ruffled his black hair. Although dawn was streaking the sky, he looked as elegant and glittering as if he had just left the hands of his valet. He did not look like the handsome rake he was reputed to be. He looked tall and dependable and overwhelmingly attractive.

She had a sudden vision of what it would be like to come home to *him,* to be folded in his arms, a still rock in a stream of shifting, chattering, glittering society.

Her hand rose to her lips to stifle a sob and she turned and went into the house.

The Marquess of Standish was pacing up and down his bedroom, still fully clothed, still disheveled.

He was no longer in the depths of despair. Harriet Comfort had told him that the Chinese were protégées of Barrington and that she would take him to Barrington on the morrow. Mad hope of seeing Li again, hope of returning to that magic world, had kept him from sleep.

But he felt an acute stab of guilt as his grave-faced wife asked him quietly to explain his conduct, to explain what he had been doing at Harriet Comfort's after he had sworn he had not seen her.

"It was the truth, my sweeting," said the Marquess earnestly. "But I have been . . . gambling . . . and am again indebted to Barrington,

I was in despair because I could not find him at his offices. I felt wretched and could not tell you the fool I had made of myself. Harriet knows the whereabouts of Barrington. Once she had told me, I was able to become calm and think rationally. I was ashamed to tell you because you had already bailed me out. . . ."

"My parents bailed you out," sighed Lucy. "I lied to them. I told them I needed a vast amount of money for a court dress. Oh, Guy, I *cannot* ask them again. But I am so happy that it was only gambling that kept you away at nights. We have become so estranged." She held out her arms. "But of course I forgive you. All we need to do is retrench. We can move to Standish . . ."

"Don't talk fustian," said the Marquess, turning his back on her. Lucy's arms fell to her side. "I would die of boredom in the country. Look, ask your papa to sport some more blunt. *He* won't miss it." He turned back and his voice became coaxing. "I know we have made a false start in this arranged marriage of ours. . . ."

"Arranged!" Lucy's hand felt for a chair back to steady herself.

"Oh, you know your parents' ambitions. Mr. Hyde-Benton paid quite a lot for my title as well you know so . . ."

His voice faltered and died at the look of blind shock on Lucy's face.

"Well, you *did* know," he said with false joviality.

Lucy dumbly shook her head.

"Well, I mean, by George, you must have *guessed*. I mean, that a man of my standing would . . . Oh, don't look *so*, Lucy. Arranged marriages happen all the time." He was all of a sudden desperate to placate her. Nothing must prevent his returning to Li. "We rub along very well, don't we? I don't interfere with your pleasures. What you need is a brat to take your mind off things."

"And how is that to be achieved, sirrah?" said his wife icily. "Another immaculate conception?"

"You funny little thing." He laughed. "You're jealous and I have not had you in my bed for a long time. Come to me!"

He held out his arms.

Lucy looked at his flushed, swollen face, at his hair damp with sweat which fell about his collar, at the wine stains on his cravat, and took two steps back and stood with her hand on the handle of the door.

"Don't *touch* me!" she spat. "Don't *ever* touch me again, Guy. If you had told me at the beginning that it was to be an arranged marriage, I would never have married you. Now I know I need no longer be faithful to you. I shall take a lover."

"You!" laughed her husband. "Miss Prunes and Prisms. That's rich, that is!"

Lucy turned and slammed the door on his jeering face.

The savage ringing of the bell from my lady's rooms sounded only minutes later. Wilson, the butler, wearily climbed back into his livery. He would need to change his bet in the betting books at the Three Feathers tavern, where the odds on the Standishes' divorce were running fifty to one before word of this night's happenings got abroad. The odds would drop to five to one in no time at all.

My lady, attired in a walking gown of severe gray wool merino, called out the carriage again and demanded to be taken to the home of the Duke of Habard. The well-trained servants murmured, "Very good, my lady," as if it was all the most ordinary thing in the world, and then returned to the kitchens to mull over the latest gossip and administer sal volatile to the cook who had gone into strong hysterics, being of a Delicate Constitution and not so hardened to the vices of high society as some she could mention.

The Duke of Habard received the intelligence that Lady Standish was awaiting him belowstairs with his usual imperturbable calm, although it was five in the morning and he had only just fallen asleep.

He did not immediately leap from bed but lay with his hands clasped behind his head, staring at the canopy and debating whether to call an end to the farce.

He had been sure when he had left her that

that would be the end of the matter. It was, he realized wryly, because he could not imagine any man turning his back on Lucy Standish.

After some time, he rang for his Swiss and gave orders to be barbered and his clothes laid out. Word was to be sent to the stables to have his traveling carriage made in readiness.

Word was to be sent to Lady Standish's residence with instructions to her lady's maid to present herself at the Duke's with her mistress's trunks.

Now I have done it, he thought, noticing the shocked look on his valet's face.

He made a leisurely toilet and descended to the morning room an hour later to find the Marchioness of Standish fast asleep by the fire. He had passed Lady Standish's grim-faced and weary lady's maid who was sitting sentinel in the hall beside several corded trunks. He had ordered his butler to supply the maid with tea and to see that the baggage was strapped onto his carriage along with his own trunks.

He stood looking down at Lucy as she sat asleep in a winged chair. She had taken her hat off and her small face was tilted back against one of the wings. She looked little more than a child.

As if aware of his gaze, her eyes flew open and she stared up at him, first in bewilderment and then in dawning comprehension.

"I had to come," she said faintly. "He does not love me. He said . . . he said my parents had *paid* him to marry me."

"It is not unusual," he said calmly. "You will breakfast. I have sent for your maid and your clothes."

"You mean . . . I will live here with you?"

"No. Nothing so blatant. You are coming to the country with me . . . to my home."

"Oh," said Lucy weakly.

"We do not want to give your husband outright grounds for divorce and so it will all be very respectable. My mother, the Dowager Duchess of Habard, is in residence."

"What will she think . . . ?"

"What she wishes. It need not concern us."

Lucy was still too tired and hurt and emotionally buffeted to protest.

When they left, a thin brown rain was falling from a low brown sky.

"Where do you live?" asked Lucy sleepily.

"Mullford Hall in Essex. It is not a very long journey so we will not have to spend the night anywhere."

Lucy's lady's maid, Harper, sat grimly opposite, holding my lady's jewel box on her lap and trying to keep the disapproval she felt at these strange goings-on from showing on her face.

The matter of Lucy's marriage could not be discussed in the presence of the maid, and after a little while, Lucy fell fast asleep, only awakening when they stopped for luncheon.

Dusk came early on that dismal day and the carriage lamps had been lit as they finally turned in at the great gates of Mullford Hall.

"Is your mama expecting me?" asked Lucy, becoming nervous despite her fatigue.

"No. It will be a surprise."

"I would rather she had been prepared," said Lucy in a small voice.

"Well, that was not possible since I was not prepared myself," said the Duke equably.

Lucy fell silent, rubbing at the steamy glass of the carriage and trying to see out the windows through the gathering twilight.

"It looks very big . . . the park, I mean," she ventured at last.

He nodded and seemed absorbed in his thoughts. Finally the carriage rattled to a stop and Lucy was helped down and stood looking up at the great pile that was Mullford Hall.

The house was Palladian in principle, consisting of a central oval building surmounted by a dome joined to two rectangular pavilions by curving wings.

"The west pavilion has not been completed," said the Duke. "We use the east, and the central building is reserved for guests. Since you are our only guest, you will share the family wing."

Lucy was led off by the housekeeper down a long corridor lined with statues and glass cases containing priceless china over to the east wing.

Her rooms were tasteful and cool with high ceilings, Adam fireplaces, and pastel walls. No sounds penetrated from the world outside.

London seemed very far away and, for the moment, her marriage ceased to exist.

It was soothing to look forward to a quiet family evening. She imagined the Dowager Duchess a tall, elegant figure — for surely that was the sort of mother the Duke would have.

At last, a vastly imposing Groom of the Chambers arrived to escort her to the Long Gallery where she was told everyone was assembled.

It seemed more like a Royal procession to Lucy as she followed the imposing back of the Groom of the Chambers, who held his tall staff with all the swagger of a Macaroni. One footman carrying a candle in a flat stick supported her on one side, and on the other, another footman with her shawl, her fan, and her vinaigrette.

Lucy stopped at the entrance of the Long Gallery with a little gasp of dismay. The Duke had only mentioned his mother. He had obviously not seen fit to include the names of several members of the county, the rector, various cousins, and three old and moth-eaten hounds.

The company arose at her entrance and the Duke led her around, making the introductions in his easy manner. Lucy's eyes flew from face to face. Which was the Dowager Duchess? As if in answer to her unspoken question, the Duke said, "Mama is late as usual. She does it quite deliberately, of course."

Lucy felt a pang of disquiet. Her feeling of

escape was melting away, leaving her with the uneasy feeling that she should be at home with her husband, no matter what he had done. She had, she realized, been hoping for some lady of mature wisdom who would comfort and counsel her. Again her conscience gave a sharp twinge. She should turn to her own mother. But her mother was so obsessed with the glamor of a title that she would simply not listen. All these thoughts were churning through Lucy's shining fair head as she murmured pleasantries to the various guests.

"I don't know why Angela cannot be on time for once," grumbled an elderly, choleric-looking gentleman called Sir Frederick Barrister, whose high starched cravat cut into the florid flesh of his fat cheeks.

"Oh, you know Mama's little ways," said the Duke of Habard soothingly. "I tell *her* dinner is at seven, don't you see, and I tell my chef to arrange it for seven-thirty, and that way the kitchen staff is not thrown into disorder."

The Groom of the Chambers rapped his staff and announced portentously from the doorway leading to the Long Gallery:

"Her Most Noble Grace, The Dowager Duchess of Habard!"

Chapter Six

The Groom of the Chambers stood aside and the Duchess stood poised on the threshold, her eyes darting around the room.

She was tiny and grotesque. Her wrinkled face was rouged and powdered like a mask. Her diaphanous, highwaisted gown revealed a pair of perfect — perfectly improbable — breasts. They were, in fact, wax. The gown was cut low and the upper half of them gleamed palely in the candlelight. She wore a frivolous little lace cap adorned with multicolored ribbons on top of a blond wig. Her pale blue, slightly pro-truding eyes fastened almost greedily on her son as she moved forward to take his arm, baring a mouthful of china teeth.

"Now, you are about to scold me, naughty boy," she cooed. "But you shall take me into dinner and then I shall know I am forgiven."

"Much as I do not wish to forego the honor, Mama," said the Duke, "my guest, Lady Standish, has the prior claim."

"Who's she?" demanded his mother rudely, her eyes raking around the room.

The Duke went across the room and took Lucy by the hand and led her forward. Lucy sank into a low curtsy while the Duchess looked down at all that beauty and youth and innocence with her face setting into a petulant mask.

"There is no need to stoop so low." She laughed shrilly, rapping Lucy playfully on the head with her fan but with such force that she snapped one of the sticks of her fan on the jewelled comb which held Lucy's blond ringlets in place.

"Now, let me see . . . Standish," the Duchess went on, beginning to rap the handle of her fan against the china of her false teeth with an alarming series of clicks.

"Pon rep, I have it now. Dev'lishly handsome buck. So he married you, heh? And where is my lord?"

"In Town, an it please Your Grace."

"It does not please me *at all*. He was a great flirt of mine. All the bucks are. Why isn't he here?"

"He may join us in a few days," interrupted the Duke smoothly. "Sir Frederick, will you oblige me by taking Mama into dinner? Your arm, Lady Standish."

Lucy's heart sank to the points of her little kid shoes as the Dowager Duchess led the way, tossing venomous glances over her shoulder.

The Duke took the head of the long table and his mother took her place at the other end — to Lucy's relief. She herself was placed next to the Duke with an ebullient young man called Harry Brainchild on her other side.

115

"Are *all* these people house guests?" asked Lucy in a low voice.

"A few cousins and aunts, I believe," said the Duke carelessly. "You are not eating, Lady Standish."

"I . . . I am still fatigued. And . . . and I fear your mother does not approve of me."

"I think you will find this Moselle to your taste," said the Duke. "If this weather lifts, I shall be able to take you riding tomorrow."

"Thank you," said Lucy meekly, wishing however that he had not deliberately ignored the remark about his mother.

Harry Brainchild promptly engaged her attention, and finding she knew nothing of the surrounding countryside, launched enthusiastically into an exhaustive description of every bird, bush, tree, animal, and fish in the surrounding district. He professed himself to be a great Lover of Nature and then went on to describe how many foxes he had killed, how many birds he had shot, and how many otter cubs he had put to death, and this history of carnage went on so long that he had, it seemed, finally paused for breath when the Dowager Duchess arose to her feet indicating that the ladies should rise also and leave the gentlemen to their wine.

It seemed to Lucy as if all the other ladies followed the Duchess's example. They clustered around her on the road to the drawing room, pointedly ignoring Lucy.

The drawing room was the one room in the house where the Duke's austere and elegant taste had not been allowed a foothold. It was dominated by a full-length portrait of the Duchess in a sky blue gown and Leghorn hat, posing before an open window which looked out onto a sky in which an approaching typhoon threatened. Garish stripes climbed up and down the walls and furniture, reminding Lucy of the interior decoration of her own townhouse. The air was suffocatingly warm and scented with patchouli. One half of the room had broken out in a rash of chinoiserie with carved dragons, silk screens, and jade buddhas, and the other half was in the new Egyptian style with Recamier couches and an enormous fireplace with carved glass sphinxes on the pilasters.

There was, however, very little light in the room. Perhaps the Dowager was conscious of her wrinkles and did not want to parade them in a blaze of candlelight.

Lucy retired quietly to a corner of the room and picked up a book of poetry, while the chatter of the ladies, grouped around the Duchess who was lying on a couch by the fire, rose and fell.

One faded cousin called Bella Bly was undulating around the sofa on which the Duchess lay as if about to perform the dance of the seven veils. She waved her arms expressively, although her arm movements had nothing to do with her conversation. Bella was describing how to make a solution which would remove the ugly effects of sunburn. "Use twenty parts of white vaseline to five parts of bismuth carbonate with three parts of Kaolin," she was saying enthusiastically, while all the time her arms and long, thin tapering fingers acted out another tale, and her deep-set haunted eyes looked down on the Duchess like Andromache seeing Hector's body bound to the victor's chariot, approaching over the plain, under the walls of Troy.

"I have no need for such ointments," said the Duchess petulantly. "My skin is perfect. Lady Standish, on the other hand, might be glad of your remedies."

Lucy kept her eyes fixed on her book. She felt to acknowledge such a remark would only bring down more bitchery upon her head.

Four lines of verse seemed to leap out of the page.

O, Western wind, when wilt thou blow,
That the small rain down can rain?
Christ, that my love were in my arms
And I in my bed again!

Her present plight had nothing to do with the anonymous voice of the Elizabethan poet, but the intense longing of the lines hit her jumbled emotions like a hammer blow, bringing with it an intense longing for freedom to love and be loved, home, children, friends, security.

And then the gentlemen joined the ladies.

She looked up from the page, her eyes wide and very dark, mirroring her loneliness and youth.

The Duke caught his breath and took a half-step forward.

"Simon!" called his mother shrilly. "We are of a mind to have a romp."

"And I am in no mood for cushion throwing. Come, Mama," admonished the Duke. "You are always putting up romps and a great deal of cushions are thrown and a great deal of glass is broken while you never remove from your couch. I can see Miss Bly is anxious to entertain us."

With many wild gestures, Miss Bella Bly headed for the pianoforte where an elderly aunt was already sifting through sheets of music.

The Duchess pouted and hunched a shriveled shoulder and then began to talk very loudly to Sir Frederick Barrister about the despair of a mother who was young at heart and who was cursed with a son who was as old as the grave.

"There is a lady sweet and kind," warbled Bella while her hands and arms put ashes on her head and sackcloth on her body.

The Duke walked over and stood by Lucy, who looked up at him with blind eyes, the poetry book lying open on her lap.

"I would like to retire," she whispered.

He nodded and held out his arm as she arose, the book slipping unnoticed to the floor.

"I will say goodnight to your mother," said Lucy nervously.

"It is not necessary to speak to anyone other than me," he said, smiling down at her in such a way that her legs trembled.

The dark blue silk of his evening coat made his metallic eyes seem almost blue. A sapphire winked in the snowy folds of his cravat and the fine frill of his shirt was almost transparent. His very elegance, Lucy reflected, seemed to set him apart. It was hard to believe he had ever kissed her. The long corridor was faintly lit by shaded oil lamps which cast little islands of golden light. China and glass shimmered softly in the shadows. A strand of ivy tapped at one of the windows.

"The wind is rising," he said. "The rain should be gone by tomorrow."

"How long shall I stay?" Her voice was very faint, almost a whisper.

"I shall be here for two weeks," he said. "After that, we will see. After a few days, perhaps it would be as well if you write to your husband. . . ."

"No!"

"*Write* to your husband and tell him where you are. The servants will have, no doubt, already told him."

"As you will."

"You sound like a tired but obedient child.

Don't look so gloomy, Lucy. Things always look better in the morning."

"But your mother, the Dowager Duchess — I fear she does not welcome my presence."

"She will do as she is bid, never fear."

"But I would rather someone were not *bidden* to tolerate me."

"Mama has to be bidden to tolerate anyone who is not precisely old and ugly. No, not another word."

They had reached the door of her apartment. He opened it for her and ushered her into her sitting room.

"How very hot it is!" said Lucy nervously. She went to the window and tugged it up a few inches from the bottom. A warm, garden-scented wind rushed into the room, sending the curtains billowing about her.

He came to stand beside her.

"There is no question of you being compromised while you are under my roof," he said gently. "Were you worried about that?"

"Yes . . . no," said Lucy, hypnotized by the long curve of his mouth.

A strand of hair blew across her mouth and he gently lifted it away, his fingers brushing her lips.

Her lips trembled and her bosom rose and fell rapidly. "What shocked you . . . startled and upset you . . . just before I came into the drawing room? Did Mama say something?"

"No," said Lucy. "It was nothing. Just a poem."

"Which one? By whom?"

"It's anonymous. Oh, a silly thing to upset me so. Something about the west wind and being back home in bed."

"Ah," he said slowly. "And do you wish you were back in your bed again with your love in your arms? Do you miss him already, Lucy? That husband of yours?"

"No. But I feel strange. It . . . the poem I mean . . . made me long for security. It is hard to think longingly of home. It was never mine, you know. We never furnished it together, Guy and me. It was all ready when I arrived, all dull and striped and soulless. And all those clocks! I never want to hear a clock again!"

As if in malice, the little gilt clock on the mantlepiece began to chime.

"You are so close . . . you stand so close," went on Lucy breathlessly. "You are so tall, you see. I have to crane my neck to see your face."

He lifted her up and swung her onto a footstool and smiled at her. "There! Now we are almost of a size."

His lashes were very long and curling. She had not noticed that before. The eyes looking into her own seemed as gray and fathomless as the North Sea. The breeze from the garden made her flimsy skirts billow about her legs and the escaping tendrils of her hair formed a sort of golden aureole about her face.

"I think I should leave . . . now," he said slowly. He put out one long finger and lightly brushed her cheek. "How you tremble," he said huskily. "Do I frighten you, Lucy?"

"I frighten myself," she said in a low voice.

He caught her abruptly to him and kissed her. All his cool elegance had gone. His lips were burning down on hers, and raw, scarlet, flaming passion seared between them, fusing their bodies and lips and minds. Her body arched itself under his, every nerve screaming for further intimacy, the ultimate intimacy.

And then just as abruptly, he put her from him, lifting her down from the footstool and setting her a little away.

"I said I would not compromise you," he said harshly, "But 'fore God, it's hard. I must go."

"Where?" said Lucy, stretching out her arms, all restraint gone.

"I am going to my bed to bite my pillow and scream," he said. And with that he marched to the door. And then he was gone.

Lucy stood shivering. She wanted to cry out with frustration. To run after him. But there was Guy, always Guy. And she was married to him, for richer, for poorer, for better, and oh, how very much for the worse!

Unknown to Lucy, the Duke had sent a very punctilious note to the Marquess of Standish before they had departed London, informing his lordship that Lady Standish was visiting Mullford Hall in Essex as a guest of the Dowager Duchess of Habard.

To any man in his right mind, this would be only so much flannel to cover up the fact that his wife had fled home in the middle of the night to seek comfort in another man's arms. But the Marquess was not in his right mind. He assumed Lucy had gone off on a highly respectable visit in a fit of the sulks. All he felt was relief. Now he could concentrate on finding Li with no guilty twinges caused by his wife's sorrowful face to slow him down. The fact that Barrington refused to see him for several days only increased his fever.

He gambled heavily and drank deep to pass the time and did not care if he was becoming the talk of London, unaware that it was his wife who was causing all sorts of startled rumors to fly around.

Servants talk to other servants and other servants confide in their masters and soon the whole of London society knew that the Marchioness of Standish had had a blazing row with her husband and had left London at dawn with the Duke of Habard to visit his home in the country. The fact that everyone knew his mother to be in residence caused even more raised eyebrows. For it looked as if the Duke's intentions might be honorable, and yet who could have honorable intentions when the lady was already married?

Finally the day of his appointment arrived, and fortified with a breakfast of brandy and water, the Marquess made his way to Mr.

Barrington's chambers in Fetter Lane.

He was startled to find four other gentlemen already there. There was Jerry Carruthers, a well-known Corinthian, then there was young Harry Chalmers, and the Earl of Oxtead, and Sir Percival Burke. He had caroused with them all at one time or the other, and noticed that they all looked about as under the weather as he felt himself.

"Now we are all here," said Mr. Barrington as the Marquess joined the group.

"I will be frank with you. All of you owe me a considerable amount of money."

"Not I," said the Marquess quickly. "My debt is paid."

Mr. Barrington smiled. "You contracted other debts, my lord."

"Well, you'll need to wait for those," said the Marquess breezily. "It ain't as if you can drag me to Bow Street and admit you're running a Chinese bawdy house."

Mr. Barrington extracted several slips of paper. "You will find, my lord, that these bills of yours, these vowels, are all made out to me for money lent to you. No mention of anything so fantastic as a . . . er . . . Chinese bawdy house. What are you going to tell the magistrate? Who will believe you? Can you take the parish-constable to this place?"

The Marquess bit his lip, thinking of the deserted tenement. Then his all-consuming desire to see Li again made him shrug and say with a smile, "I see you have me there, Barrington."

All the Marquess wanted was to find Li. Then he could prove Barrington's villainy. But only after he had had Li. That was all that mattered.

Nonetheless, he asked to see the vowels, feeling quite ill when he realized how he had been tricked. These were the slips of paper he had so cheerfully signed in the opium den without examining them. Barrington had tricked him out of a vast sum of money.

"Now," said Barrington in his fatherly voice, "I could ruin *all* of you." Five pairs of eyes burned with hate. "Yes, all of you. But I am prepared to tear up all your debts for one small service which only one of you need perform. You will draw straws to see who will be the lucky man. The rest of you will sign papers to say that you were part of the plot. These papers will never be used against you . . . unless you talk."

"Well, what is it?" drawled Sir Percival Burke pettishly. "What *small* service?"

"One of you," said Mr. Barrington cheerfully, "has to kill Mr. Benjamin Wilkins."

"You're mad," said the Marquess hoarsely. "Kill the Prime Minister. In god's name, *why?*"

"Personal reasons," said Mr. Barrington, his good humor unimpaired. "And now I will leave you to discuss it among yourselves. May I remind you that I will ruin each and every one of you should even one of you refuse."

With that, he waddled from the room. The

five men looked at each other in silence.

Then they all started talking at once. It was monstrous, *evil*. They would band together and inform the authorities. But after a few moments, their vehemence abated. The Marquess thought bitterly that in order to pay Barrington, he would need to turn over most of his estates. And bad landlord though he was, the whole thing seemed impossible.

As for the others, it transpired that Barrington was able to blackmail each and every one of them, apart from ruining them financially. He held letters and information of their amorous exercises which would damn them socially for life. Each was married and their wives, unlike Lucy, were unaware of their infidelities.

"Why does he want old Wilkins out of the way?" asked the Marquess.

"Wanted a peerage," said Sir Percival gloomily. "Wilkins said over his dead body. Barrington has his sights set on Wilkins's replacement, the Prince Regent's man, James Erskine, and Erskine's promised him a baronetage."

"Oh, *God*," said the Marquess, burying his throbbing head in his hands. "We can't take this seriously. We mustn't."

"Oh, I don't know," said Mr. Jerry Carruthers. "There's a lot would be glad to see old Wilkins dead. He's mining the economy. He's practically in his grave anyway. And we're all of a social position to get close enough to pot a shot at him without anyone knowing who fired it."

They argued and argued but at last it was decided that they would need to go through with it. They were five weak and very desperate men.

Mr. Barrington did not seem in the least surprised at the nods of assent when he reentered the room.

With fast-beating heart, the Marquess drew first. And then he let out a sigh of relief. A long straw.

It was young Jerry Carruthers who drew the shortest straw and the Marquess privately thought he was the best man for the job. There had been unsavory stories about Carruthers's cruelty during his nighttime carousing, raping young servant girls being the mildest of his exploits.

"When?" was all Jerry Carruthers asked as he stared down at the straw in his hand.

"As soon as possible," said Barrington jovially. "And now, gentlemen, if you will all sign this paper . . . then you shall reclaim your vowels . . . and er . . . certain letters . . . certain *scented* letters. . . ."

The Marquess waited impatiently for the others to leave and then he faced Barrington.

"Li," he said.

"Ah, yes," said Mr. Barrington. "The fascinating Li. I suppose you deserve it." He scribbled something on a piece of paper and passed it over. "Here. Look on it as a present. I am a generous man to my friends."

The Marquess seized the paper and looked down at the bill broker who was leaning back in his chair behind the desk, his hands clasped over his waistcoat.

"Do not dare to call me friend," said the Marquess haughtily. "You are scum, and worse than scum. You will not even commit the crime yourself."

"How you do crow on your dunghill, my little cock," said Barrington, his jovial mask slipping. "You talk of scum, you and your fine friends who dare to sneer at *me*. But soon I shall be one of you, soon I shall be my Lord Barrington, and *no one* is going to stop me . . . least of all a callow drunken youth who loses his wife to another man before the marriage is a year old."

The Marquess opened his mouth to retort, but he had Li's address and if he stayed to insult this old criminal further, then Barrington might make the magical Li disappear again.

He turned and ran.

The long evening shadows were creeping across the lawns of Mullford Hall. It had been a blustery chilly day to remind the English that long hot summers belonged to foreigners and other more fortunate people. It would have been a perfect day for riding but news of the Duke's arrival had spread throughout the country and he was besieged all day by farmers and tenants and visitors. Lucy was left to her own devices.

She had walked through the gardens, had been taken on a tour of the hothouses by the Scotch head gardener, and had kept as far away from the Dowager Duchess as possible.

Now it was time to prepare for dinner and her heart beat hard at the thought of seeing the Duke again. She would not admit to herself the reasons for the strength of her feelings. She told herself cynically that she was flattered to have so important and so powerful a friend. It was only her nervous insecurity and inexperience which had made her respond so ardently to his kisses.

But her heart plunged when she entered the Long Gallery and found him absent. Bella Bly was there along with the Duchess and three elderly cousins and a brace of aunts. Harry Brainchild had been joined by three Tom and Jerrys from London and Lucy recognized two of her husband's friends. But either they did not recognize her or they were too absorbed in bragging of their sporting exploits, but in any case they paid her only the scantest attention.

Lucy thought them strange friends for the elegant and fastidious Duke to have until it transpired from the conversation that the Duchess had asked them. She treated them to a grotesque parody of a shy but flirtatious debutante at her first Season.

Lucy found herself wondering what the Duke thought of his mother and whether her behavior had stopped him from becoming married. Any bride would surely have little say in the running of Mullford Hall or in the choosing of the guests.

With the Duke still absent, the three Corinthians set the tone of the dinner and a very vulgar tone it was too. They flattered the Duchess shamelessly and told stories which were warm, to say the least. Lucy found her skin prickling with embarrassment. She had enough Town bronze to know that if she should show the slightest disapproval or embarrassment, it would only encourage these appalling young men to further efforts.

The slender dining chairs creaked as they flung their bulk back against the spars in fits of hearty laughter. The Duchess was drinking a great deal and becoming more flushed and animated by the minute.

There was no help from the aunts and cousins who took their cue from the Duchess and shrieked and tittered and exclaimed in a quite horribly sycophantic manner.

It came as almost no surprise when the gentlemen agreed to take their port in the drawing room with the ladies. There was nothing they could now say, thought Lucy, which had not already been said. She had often wondered what gentlemen talked about when the ladies had retired, and now she knew.

The Duchess was very tipsy. Her wig — red this time — was askew and one of her false breasts had slipped around under her left armpit.

"We'll have no caterwauling tonight," she said maliciously as Bella headed for the piano-forte. "We'll have a romp. We'll *eat* Lady Standish!"

To Lucy's horror, her grace removed her false china teeth and held them out in her hand, making snapping noises in the back of her throat.

Lucy sprang behind the sofa as the party shrieked with glee and began to gnash their teeth in mock rage.

It was like a nightmare. The flickering candles seemed to make the glistening faces dance and shimmer. Shadows flew up the walls to the painted ceiling as Lucy darted hither and thither, crying breathlessly, "Stop. Oh, do *stop!*"

Harry Brainchild made a dart in Lucy's direction and went flying over a footstool and nearly ended up in the fire.

"Good evening."

The chill accents of the Duke of Habard acted like a douche of cold water on the room. The Duchess quickly put her teeth back in and sank down onto the sofa in her usual pose.

The cousins and aunts, who had been so many withered and menacing demons a bare moment before, were immediately transformed into faded and shame-faced elderly ladies. The men stood at attention as if at a military lineup.

"We were just having a romp," said Bella Bly breathlessly while her arms waved like a windmill.

"Indeed!" said the Duke icily. "Mama, in future you will consult me in the matter of which guests you choose to invite to *my* home. I see Lady Standish is looking fatigued. I will escort her to her apartments and then I shall retire myself.

"I have had a fatiguing day. I am sorry I shall not have time to talk to you gentlemen since you will have left early in the morning before I am about. I shall give the servants orders to pack your trunks. Do feel free to visit me again should I ever extend such an invitation. And you, my dear relations, I am sure your families must be missing you sorely since you have been away from them so long. I urge you to think of them and return as soon as possible. Lady Standish . . . *if* you please."

Lucy followed him silently from the room.

"If you will fetch your cloak, Lady Standish," he said with chilly formality, "we will take the air. The atmosphere this evening is suffocating."

"Have I offended you?" asked Lucy timidly.

"Never," he said with a quick smile.

"You called me Lady Standish."

"Ah, I was trying to make up for my family's lack of formality by showing a little of it myself. Collect your cloak and bonnet, Lucy."

He waited punctiliously outside her rooms until she emerged wrapped in a long blue cloak with a hood.

The night was clear and bright with moonlight, and full of the sounds of rushing wind. Ragged wisps of cloud flew across the sky and a small whirpool of rose petals danced at the bottom of the wide, shallow stone steps that led down into the shelter of the walled gardens.

The air was quite warm out of the rush of the wind.

Lucy's long skirts made a soft swishing sound on the grass and her fair hair gleamed silver in the moonlight.

"I do not normally discuss my mother," he said with a sigh. "But she has become eccentric to the point of madness. My father was a gentle, retiring, scholarly man. I am more like my grandfather. No one knows my mother's background. My father claimed she was Scotch, and certainly he returned with her on his arm after a visit to that country. But I learned as I grew older that my mother was not even sure whereabouts Scotland was in the geography of the British Isles.

"It was rumored she came from a very low background and my father had done all in his power to eradicate any traces of it. She was exceptionally beautiful. When I was a child, she seemed like a fairy princess to me — on the few occasions that I saw her. But the vulgar behavior which was forgiven because of her delicate beauty began to seem more horrible as her looks faded. Father died when I was still in shortcoats, and then Mama began to entertain day and night. I swear she would still take lovers if she could. Only the quick deterioration of her looks put a stop to her immorality. But I have allowed her too much license. She has been warned that she is shortly expected to remove to the Dower House where she may entertain whom she will. She will extend an invitation to anyone who will toady to her and I am heartily sick of toadies. Poor Lucy. This is not the calm refuge I would have wished to offer you."

"Is that why you have never married?" asked Lucy shyly.

His eyes glinted down at her in the moonlight. "No," he said. "Mama did not turn me against your sex. I simply have not been in love."

"Oh," said Lucy sadly.

"You need not feel sorry for me. I have felt passion for many women in my time, but alas, it does not last very long."

"Oh," said Lucy again. She tried to fight against the wave of depression that was engulfing her. So she was just another passionate episode in his life. A fleeting emotion.

"Did you write to your husband?" he asked, turning his head away from her.

"Yes. Today."

"And do you think he will come?"

"I don't know," said Lucy wretchedly, wishing disloyally and all at once that she weren't married. If the strange Guy of the past weeks still existed, then he would not come. If the old fashion-hungry Guy was back again, then he would. But she could not bring herself to say this.

All she said bleakly was, "He does not love me."

"Love comes in many forms," he said harshly. "It is not all like poems and novels. I think you will find your husband loves you . . . in his fashion."

"Perhaps."

"Then let us retire. I will be better situated to entertain you tomorrow. And most of the unwelcome guests should be gone. Bella is the only one who lives with us permanently and she is kind in her way."

"Yes."

The Duke came closer to her, his bulk a blacker blackness in the dark garden. The air was suddenly charged with tension. Lucy's whole body seemed to lean towards him.

But he gently drew her arm through his and led her back to the house, back to her apartments, where he bade her a courteous goodnight.

The passionate man who had burned in her arms the night before seemed to have gone forever.

The human body was a treacherous beast, reflected Lucy bitterly as her maid prepared her for bed. Did Guy throb and burn for Harriet Comfort? If he did, then he was to be much pitied. Or was there some other woman, some other *demimondaine* or Fashionable Impure who had made him forget his marriage vows so soon?

The Marquess of Standish stirred uneasily in his sleep and then finally awoke. A shaft of sunlight was struggling through the grimy panes of a curtainless window somewhere above his head.

And then he remembered.

Li!

Vague memories of his night of ecstacy twisted lazily in his fogged brain. He propped himself up on one elbow and looked down at the girl sleeping next to him.

Her black hair was tumbled over the greasy pillow and the faint lemon of her skin showed through the patches of white paint on her face. Her naked body was thin to the point of emaciation.

The room smelled abominably of stale opium fumes, brandy, and the stench from the kennel outside. Her glittering garments were folded carefully over a chair. The sunlight revealed the jewels to be made of paste and the brocade to be far from clean.

This could not be his enchantress of the night? This half-starved child.

"Li!" he said urgently.

She opened one almond eye and looked at him.

"Wot is it, guv?" she demanded crossly. "Can't a girl get a bit o' sleep?"

"You are not Chinese!" he exclaimed, hearing the Cockney accents of Bow.

"Oh, Lor'." Li came fully awake. "I waren't s'posed to speak. 'I'll 'ave your guts fer garters an you do,' says old Barrington. I'm Chinese all right, but I was born 'ere, see. 'Them flash culls,' says Mr. Barrington, 'likes for to think they're mountin' a bit o' the magic Orient. So keep your chatterbox closed or I'll make over your phiz,' 'e says, says 'e, rotten old 'oremaster that 'e is. You won't tell 'im, there's a luv?"

The Marquess dumbly shook his head. He staggered to his feet and started slowly and painfully putting on his clothes while all the while his bloodshot blue eyes raked around the sordid room.

Oh, the wonders of candlelight and opium! What had seemed a mystic temple the night before was now revealed as a dingy basement room with peeling plaster walls.

"I must go," he said dully.

Li wound a dirty wrapper around her thin body and trotted over to help him with his coat.

"You won't tell old Barrington?" she repeated anxiously.

He shook his head.

"Well, *that's* all right," said Li cheerfully. "So

if you're off, you're off, as the beadle said to the nursery maid. I'm goin' back to bed."

The Marquess raised his hand wearily in farewell and stumbled out of the door and up the steps.

Hammers were thudding in his brain. A fresh wind was blowing and above the jumbled tenements and shop signs and gin shops and chimneys was a clear blue sky.

He had such a revulsion of the soul that he thought he would be sick.

His self-respect was in ruins. He searched in his tail pocket for his watch and found it had gone. He searched in his other pockets for his money and found that had gone also.

With a muttered exclamation, he was about to turn and go back. As she had helped him into his coat Li's busy little hands had also relieved him of his possessions.

But the thought of facing that sordid scene again made him shudder.

He wandered on and on through the mean narrow streets, unable to call a hack since he had no money.

By the time he reached home, he was tired beyond belief. His butler seemed to be trying to tell him something but he brushed the man aside and went into his study at the back of the house. The morning papers were lying on his desk and by force of habit he found himself picking them up to scan the day's news.

The Prime Minister, Benjamin Wilkins, had been assassinated.

The room seemed to swim about him and he forced himself to concentrate on the print.

Mr. Wilkins had been at Vauxhall the night before with a party of friends. They had gone to watch the fireworks display and it was only when the display was over and the crowd thinned out that the Prime Minister had collapsed to the ground, a bullet wound in his back.

It was assumed that the shot had been fired during the display and that the sound of the fireworks had covered up the sound of the murderous shot.

For the first time since his marriage, the Marquess had an intense desire to be held in his wife's arms. He rang the bell and asked if there had been any news from her ladyship. The butler turned over a pile of correspondence and selected a letter with a heavy seal.

"You may leave," said the Marquess sharply when it appeared that the butler was going to wait to see him open it.

The letter was brief and chilly. Lucy begged to inform her husband that she was a guest of the Dowager Duchess of Habard and that he was welcome to join her if he pleased.

A faint perfume arose from the letter, bringing all Lucy's youth and freshness and innocence vividly to mind.

All at once, the Marquess decided to turn

over a new leaf. He would be the best husband London had ever seen. He would set out for Essex and, with luck, should arrive on the morrow. First, he had something to attend to. He opened a secret compartment in his desk and drew out a thick brown notebook in which he had lodged in code the names and addresses of various members of London's Fashionable Impure.

Turning to a clean page, he began to jot down in rapid code — a code he had devised for his own amusement — the names of the conspirators and all the facts of how Barrington had coerced them all into being a party to the murder.

It took him two hours of concentrated thought, and, after that, he carefully hid the book away again, mounted the stairs to his bedchamber, and fell into an exhausted sleep.

Since that evening in the garden, the Duke of Habard had been a punctilious host. His mother had retired to her rooms in a huff and Bella Bly had gone on a visit with one of the departing aunts, so it seemed as if there was nothing to mar the beauty of the house or the surrounding countryside.

Lucy and the Duke went out riding in the mornings, and, in the afternoons, he took her on a lazy walking tour of the grounds. In the evening, they dined together, talking comfortably of books and music. The Duke was warm and friendly, but not by the slightest gesture or look did he betray that his feelings for Lucy had even been anything warmer.

And Lucy, always conscious of her conscience and her married state, was able to accept him as a friend and enjoy a relatively peaceful night's sleep, untrammeled by any of the screaming frustration she had felt before. She was even able to admit to herself wryly that she might have been on the point of falling in love with the handsome Duke.

They discussed the assassination of the Prime Minister at length and finally came to the conclusion that it must have been the work of some madman. It was supposed that Mr. Erskine would be the next choice to head the coalition, and the Duke said he was too weak and shiftless a man for the job.

He came to this conclusion over breakfast, looking out at the vista of a perfect early summer's day, with thin wreaths of mist being burned away by the hot sun. He told Lucy that he had business to attend to, but if she would care, in the afternoon he would take her for a walk in the woods to a certain beauty spot, and he told her to wear some serviceable clothes.

London and Guy and all the troubles of her marriage seemed very far away as Lucy set out with him in the afternoon, wearing a blue muslin gown, half-boots, and a broad-brimmed straw hat on her head.

The Duke was wearing an old game coat,

buckskins, and a shabby pair of hunting boots. He wore a belcher scarf loosely knotted around his neck and his thick black hair had not been subjected to the usual rigors of the hairdresser's art and shone like a raven's wing in the bright sunlight.

Without his usual armor of formal elegance, he looked infinitely more human and approachable and incredibly handsome. Lucy found to her dismay that her legs had that old trembling sort of feeling as he put his arms around her waist to lift her over a fallen log, and although his touch was cool and impersonal, she could not seem to quiet the tumult of her emotions.

She was painfully aware of the intimacy of their situation, of the curve of his mouth and the caressing laughter in his eyes as he looked down at her.

Then at last he was saying, "Here is our beauty spot."

They had come upon a small round pond in the middle of the wood. The water was green and cool and sparks of sunlight glittered on its surface. The leaves of the tall trees whispered lazily above their heads in the lightest of summer breezes. A bramble bush trailed its white stars of flowers over the water.

Lucy felt a lump rising in her throat, the imperfection of her life striking her in the face of all this simplicity and perfection.

Her eyes filled with tears and the water swam

and shimmered in front of her blurred gaze.

"Ah, no, sweeting," he said softly. "I did not bring you here to make you cry."

The endearment, unexpected as it was, was too much for poor Lucy and she began to cry in earnest.

He wrapped his arms around her and buried his lips in her hair. "Don't," he whispered, his voice muffled. "Please don't."

And then she knew that she loved him. He turned her face up to his and looked long and searchingly down into her drowned blue eyes, and then he kissed her very tenderly, very slowly, and for a long time, his tongue exploring the salt taste of her wet cheeks, his lips kissing her eyes, her nose, and her mouth again.

His hands pressed her sun-warmed dress and body closely down the length of his own, feeling her breasts pressing through the thin fabric of his shirt under his open coat.

At last he drew back with a little sigh. "Alas, we cannot," he said with a rueful smile. "Who would believe that I, with my rakish reputation, would be so very, very good. But I am no marriage breaker, Lucy."

"You cannot break what was broken already," said Lucy sadly.

"You can make it irreparable," he said. "We must return to our former friendship, Lucy. I do not think you should stay very much longer. I do not think I can keep a bridle on my feelings forever."

"What are your feelings?" begged Lucy. If only he said he loved her then she would have that to remember.

But he shrugged and turned away. "Some things must never be said. Come along, Lucy. These woods are enchanted. Did you know that? We will be pixie-led if we do not hurry."

Lucy hurried to join him, making a heroic effort to match his light mood and finally succeeding as they approached the great stone edifice that was Mullford Hall.

"Why didn't I notice that swing before?" said Lucy. "Do the servants' children use it?"

"I do not know. Mama used to use it once. She used to dress — just like Marie Antoinette, if you can believe it — in shepherdess gown with panniers and carrying a crook embellished with a blue bow. She would sit on the swing and allow her court of admirers to take turns at pushing her on the swing. My father and I would watch from the library window."

"A lonely picture," said Lucy. "A small boy and his father watching a callous woman."

"You have claws, Lucy. Do not sink them into my dear mother. Some gamble, some drink, and some — like my mother — crave attention. Sit down and I will push you and see if you can catch one of the leaves up there."

The swing was hung on two ropes from the branch of an oak tree. Lucy sat on the swing and gave a gasp as she seemed to fly up in the branches, her hat falling to the ground and her golden hair tumbling about her shoulders. "Not so hard, Simon." She laughed. "Please stop. I would rather deal with any admirers sitting on a secure and unmoving sofa!"

He let the swing go and watched as Lucy swung lower and lower, the thin muslin of her dress molded against her body, her rioting tumbling hair, falling about her face, shining in the sunlight.

All of a sudden he caught the ropes of the swing and she tossed back her hair and turned a laughing face up to his.

"Oh, God help me," he said with such force that her face paled. "You enchant me."

He bent and kissed her passionately as if his whole mind and body and soul were behind that one kiss, and her mounting passion rose to her lips and answered his. And so they stayed, held by passion, fused by passion. Two still figures on a sunny landscape.

And that is how Guy, Marquess of Standish, found them.

Chapter Seven

The Marquess of Standish had ridden out from London feeling like a new man and with all his good and shining resolutions to keep him company. But as the miles fell behind, the murder of Wilkins seemed like a bad dream. And, after all, he, the Marquess, had not actually committed it.

Li and Harriet Comfort and Mr. Barrington seemed unreal on this lovely sunny day. He had meant to reach Mullford Hall by nightfall, but all of a sudden a channing ale house with a pretty garden seemed to beckon. The tavern wench was as attractive as the inn. It was not as if he had to hurry, he told himself. Barrington's sneer about losing his wife was ridiculous. Lucy had been upset, of course, and had no right to run to Habard at that shocking time of the day. But Habard had done the correct thing by taking her to his mother. Poor old Lucy, thought the Marquess with a return of some of his old malice.

She probably hoped to take Habard as a lover to make me jealous, but she picked someone too high in the instep. Poor Lucy! he thought again. The Duke would never form a *tendre* for such a schoolgirl as she. Silly little thing.

And with these comfortable thoughts, the

Marquess settled down to dally at the inn and dally with the tavern maid, and so the sun was high in the sky next day when he swung himself up onto his horse and set out once more.

Now he regretted having only brought a single change of clothes, since, at the outset, he had meant to borrow the Duke's traveling carriage and take Lucy straight home. That way he could enjoy the ride out without encumbering himself with excessive baggage and servants.

But as he approached the magnificence of Mullford Hall, he began to wish he had arrived in style. To cover up for this, he ordered the Duke's servants about very haughtily, commanding that his dusty saddlebags be unstrapped and put in his wife's rooms.

Being informed that the Duke and Lady Standish were "somewhere about the grounds," he fortified himself with two brimmers of canary and decided to find his wife before he changed. It would look more loverlike to appear before her in all his travel stains — and besides, he had only the one change of clothes and should reserve those for dinner.

He heard Lucy's voice coming from the west, borne on the breeze. She was laughing and shouting something.

He turned a corner of the west wing . . . and stopped, frozen, rooted to the spot.

As still as china figurines, the Duke and Guy's wife were locked in an embrace so passionate, so still, that not a fold of Lucy's gown moved.

All hell broke loose in the Marquess's head. This was *his* wife, his possession, as much as his lands and houses and horses. Rather than surrender an inch of his lands, he had conspired to kill the Prime Minister. To him, Lucy was in line with his other possessions.

Without pausing for thought, he strode forward. The couple broke apart; Lucy startled and white, the Duke grim.

The Marquess pulled off one of his gloves and struck the Duke across the face.

"I am returning to London with *my wife*," he spat out. "*Your* seconds may find me in town where I will furnish them with the name of my seconds. Come, Lucy."

"This is madness," said Lucy.

"Madness! To be cuckolded, madam?" He seized Lucy by the wrist and dragged her from the swing.

"I won't go," she said wildly. "Simon! Help me!"

"You must go," said the Duke gravely. "You are his wife and it is a matter of honor."

Lucy tore herself away from Guy and ran towards the house, tears streaming down her face. He did not love her. He did not want her. What was this thing about honor? She did not *understand*.

But Guy did, and he smiled slowly at the Duke before he turned away. He knew, by all the laws of society, that the Duke was in the wrong. He knew himself to be one of the best shots in England. His anger had evaporated as quickly as it had blown up and he felt elated and cocky. It would do his social prestige no harm at all to drop a hint here and there that he was dueling with the great Duke of Habard.

The old Guy was back.

The Duke stayed for a long time. The swing moved gently to and fro until he put out an impatient hand to still it.

Men may philander, women may not. They did, of course, and no one minded — that is, until they were found out.

By the laws of society, he was in the wrong and the profligate Marquess was in the right. He thought ruefully of the Marquess's renowned expertise with firearms.

Standish was insufferable. But he had been married to Lucy in church and before the eyes of God and the top ten thousand; she was his wife to do with as he pleased.

On the road back to London, Guy, seated comfortably in a corner of the Duke's well-sprung traveling carriage, berated his wife on her disgraceful behavior. It had been easy to extract the truth from Lucy that there had been no serious affair.

Feeling righteous was a new and heady experience for the Marquess and he was making the most of it.

They passed the night at an inn on the road,

the Marquess, to Lucy's relief, reserving separate bedchambers.

The next day his tirade continued. When they reached the house in Clarence Square by noon, Lucy's nerves were in shreds.

Heedless of the listening servants, she rounded on him in the hall.

"I am leaving you, my lord," she said coldly. "I have endured enough of your pompous behavior."

"Oh, no you don't," he sneered. He grabbed her arm and twisted it painfully behind her back. "You will stay locked in your room," he said, forcing her up the stairs. "And there you will wait until tonight to pleasure me like a good wife should."

"No!" spat Lucy. "Never again will you touch me!"

"There ain't nothing you can do about it, my lady." He grinned. He threw her into her room and locked the door and pocketed the key.

Lucy hammered furiously on the door. "You will not touch me," she screamed through the panels. "I will *shoot* you first. Do you hear me, Guy? I will *shoot* you first."

The Marquess laughed and sauntered down the stairs. He gave instructions to the wide-eyed servants that my lady was to be kept under lock and key. And then he left to brag around the clubs of his forthcoming duel until a friend pointed out that every one of the eight Bow Street Runners in London must have heard about it and would surely put a stop to it.

Gone, however, were all the Marquess's good resolutions. He drank and gambled and gambled and drank; until he was feeling in a fit mood to take just revenge on his wife. He stood on the steps of Watier's, pulling on his gloves and waiting for his carriage, when he espied the other four conspirators making their way along the street: Jerry Carruthers, Harry Chalmers, the Earl of Oxtead, and Sir Percival Burke.

His eyes gleaming with malice, the Marquess hailed them.

"We meet again, gentlemen," he crowed. "And if it isn't Mr. Carruthers. Well, well, well. Enter first murderer."

"Stow your gab," hissed Harry Chalmers, looking over his shoulder.

"Y'know," said the Marquess cheerfully. "We were fools to let Barrington get away with it. We could still take him."

"The deed is done, Standish," said Sir Percival. "Keep silent or it will be the worse for you."

"Are you threatening me?" demanded the Marquess truculently. "Well, it's all right for you weasels to run scurrying when Barrington snaps his fingers. But we Standishes are made of different stuff. I will tell if I feel like it or keep quiet. But it will be whichever suits *me*." He waved to his coachman. "I shall not need the carriage, John. I have decided to walk."

He grinned again at the conspirators, crammed his bicorne at a drunken angle on his fair curls, and sauntered off whistling. The four watched him go.

Ann Hartford called on Lucy Standish that evening and refused to listen to Wilson the butler's stately announcement that "my lady is not home."

"Stuff," said Ann rudely. "I saw her face at the window as I was getting down from the carriage."

"One of the chambermaids perhaps . . . ?"

"Fiddle. What is going on, Wilson?"

There came a furious banging at a door upstairs and Lucy's voice screamed, "Ann! Help me!"

Ann gave the butler a startled look and ran past him and up the stairs.

"Lucy!" she called, rattling the handle. "This door is *locked*."

"I know it's locked," called Lucy. "Guy has taken the key. Oh, you must get me out."

"Have the servants a duplicate?"

"I don't think so."

"Well, what about the door to your sitting room?"

"Ann, it's locked as well. Of *course* I tried it."

"He may have forgotten to take that key as well," said Ann. Lucy's sitting room adjoined her bedroom.

Ann ran along the corridor and smiled triumphantly as she saw the key in the lock. Lucy almost fell into her arms as she opened the door.

"Now, now," said Ann Hartford soothingly. "What is all this I hear? Guy is babbling in the clubs about you and the Duke and that he is to fight a duel with Habard. It's too nonsensical!"

"Oh, Ann it's *true*," wailed Lucy. "And I love him so."

"Guy is not worth your love."

"Not *Guy*. Simon!"

"Oh, dear," said Ann, sitting down suddenly. "This is terrible. You must not, Lucy. Habard is a charming man, but a heartbreaker. He has been philandering, that is all."

"No," said Lucy fiercely. "No."

"He said he loved you, I suppose."

"Well, n-no he didn't, Ann, but I could see. . . ."

"And he encouraged you to get a divorce?"

"Oh, no, he is much too respectable to do that."

"Really! So he kisses and hugs you or, for all I know, introduces you to the delights of his bed, and yet he is in *love* with you!"

"Stop! Stop!" said Lucy with her hands over her ears. "You make it sound so grubby."

"Enough of this. Are you frightened of Guy?"

"Yes, so very frightened. He is . . . he is going to *force* me to pleasure him as . . . as . . . revenge."

"Then you will come home with me immediately," said Ann briskly. "No, don't ring for

154

your maid. Leave everything. My servants can fetch your trunks in the morning and you shall stay with me until this ridiculous duel is over."

"There will be no duel," said Lucy. "For I am going to inform Bow Street."

"Nonsense. If either Habard or Guy found out then *neither* of them would look at you again. You do not understand gentlemen and the emphasis they put on these affairs of honor."

"Well, never mind," said Lucy. "I must leave, and quickly."

The two women crept down the stairs. The servants were all out of sight. Wilson, the butler, who had been listening at the door, had scurried away. If my lady left, it must appear to be without his knowledge.

Ann and Lucy emerged on the doorstep and were halted by an enraged shout from across the square.

The Marquess of Standish had seen them. His eyes gleaming dangerously in the flickering light of the parish lamps, he lurched toward them.

Lucy let out a little scream and clutched Ann.

And then a shot rang out. The Marquess felt a teriffic blow in his back and staggered forward. Lucy's white face seemed startlingly near and clear and then it began to blur and fade.

Making a superhuman effort, he lurched forward and fell by the steps at her feet, clutching a fold of her dress in his hand.

The house was in an uproar as servants tumbled out, shouting, "Hey, watch! Watch! Murder! Murder!" And then came the rickety clatter of the watchman's rattle at the end of the square.

Lucy knelt and pillowed Guy's head in her lap. For a moment his mind and his vision cleared. He knew he was dying, dying and leaving Lucy to Habard. He looked solemnly up into her eyes and whispered, "I love you, Lucy. D-don't m-marry anyone else."

"Oh, I won't, Guy," said Lucy with tears streaming down her face. "Of course I won't."

The Marquess gave a little smile, a little cough, and died with his head in her lap. Ann Hartford, who had caught his last words, thought bitterly that it was like the man to be as self-centered in his last gasp as he had been in his life.

For a time it seemed as if Lucy would be suspected for the murder of her husband. Had not the servants heard her shouting that she would shoot him?

But when the furor died down and the servants realized that the Marchioness had inherited everything belonging to the Marquess, and after grumbling that it sounded like a very "Scotch arrangement" since they had been sure they and the property would go to a nephew, they made a turnabout and calmed down to present the true facts of the case — namely that the Marchioness had been locked in her room all day and had been on the point of leaving with Mrs. Hartford when the Marquess had been shot.

But ugly rumors still circulated. The Marquess had said he was to fight a duel with the Duke of Habard. The Marquess was an expert shot. The Duke of Habard was in love with the Marchioness. Therefore it followed that the couple had conspired to rid themselves of the unwanted husband.

Scandal sheets appeared in the booksellers' shops with cartoons of a painted and voluptuous-looking Lucy handing the Duke a gun, and, like Lady Macbeth saying, "If it were done, when 'tis done, then 'twere well it were done quickly."

A mob began to gather in Clarence Square daily — not so many weeks after the funeral was over — to jeer the little Marchioness every time she emerged from seclusion.

Lucy had not heard from the Duke of Habard. She herself had no intention of communicating with him ever again. Guilt had struck her like a hammer blow when the dying Guy had said he loved her. As time passed and the ugly rumors persisted, Lucy began to think that the Duke might possibly have done the deed. She did not realize that she was so anxious to expunge all thoughts of him from her mind that she was ripe to believe the worst.

At last, becoming increasingly afraid of the anger of the mob, Lucy decided to retreat to Standish, the Marquess's country home that she had only seen once before.

It was when she was driving through the village of Standish that the cure to all her miseries began to take place.

Her wide eyes noticed barefoot, shabby children playing in the dust outside rundown cottage doors.

Lucy's parents, for all their social climbing, had instilled in her the basic grounding for running a country estate.

"See the land is in good heart and the tenants are clothed and fed," her father had said, "and you will have no fear of riots."

Standish itself was an old Tudor mansion which was fortunately in better repair than the village, the old Marquess having put a great deal of money into the restoration. Lucy settled down to her new role with a will, interviewing the steward and then the tenant farmers, the vicar, and the tenants themselves, and beginning to feel an easing of the pain and worry over her husband's death as she lost herself in all this activity.

The money the Marquess had milked out of the estate had been quite amazing, and with this new shattering proof of her late husband's sheer self-interest, a little of the guilt she felt over his death began to disappear.

Although the Marquess had left staggering

debts, the steward, a very sensible man called Mr. Joseph Berry, pointed out that without the immense drain on the estate caused by his lordship's bills, they should very shortly come about. Lucy gave instructions that the hunting box in Leicester was to be sold and the townhouse in Clarence Square. The proceeds from these sales were to be ploughed into the Standish estate and the estate in the north. The steward reflected there was a lot to be said for her ladyship coming from the more practical-minded middle class rather than the aristocracy. She seemed to have no interest in keeping up appearances and promptly put all her jewels up for sale.

She gave instructions that the furniture from the townhouse should be sent to Standish with the exception of the clocks. She did not think she could bear the sound of all that ticking and tocking again.

Ann Hartford arrived after Lucy had been in residence for some months, bringing her husband with her, and the intelligence that the authorities had decided the Marquess's death was the result of an attack by some footpad. She did not mention the Duke of Habard. She did, however, bring some disquieting news. Ann had agreed to supervise the carting of the furniture from Clarence Square. She said she had found that the Marquess's study had been ransacked. Papers were lying all over the floor and furniture had been overturned. It was assumed the burglars had been surprised and had not had time to take anything of value.

Two days after her arrival, Ann was seated in the cheerful, sunny morning mom, helping Lucy repair curtains for the drawing room, when she suddenly put down her sewing and said, "Lucy. I did not like to speak of this so soon after Guy's death but it has been preying on my mind. You are young and pretty — too young and pretty to be burdened with the cares of the estate."

"I have an excellent steward," said Lucy in surprise. "I told you, Ann. Without Guy taking thousands and thousands of pounds out of the exchequer of the estate, we should soon be extremely prosperous again. Did you not notice? All the houses in Standish have been repaired and the church has set up a clothes fund. And not before time. The people were so poor and ill-cared-for that they were on the point of burning Standish to the ground! How Guy could let things come to such a pass . . ."

"Well, he could and he did and he did not care a rap for anyone other than himself. Which is what I want to talk to you about. Do you remember his last words?"

"Often," said Lucy in a low voice. "To think that he *did* love me."

"Fiddle! That young man was selfish to the last — and his last dying thought was that you should not be happy!"

"Oh, no," said Lucy, her eyes filling with

tears. "He *must* have meant it."

"Oh, Lucy, I would not hurt you for worlds, but did he ever do anything in the short span of your marriage that showed he cared one rap for you?"

Lucy thought. She remembered Guy saying her parents had bought his title, she remembered his infidelity, his lies, his gambling, and his drunkenness. And she then remembered the times he appeared warm and caring.

"Oh, I don't know. I can't think," she said wretchedly.

"You see, there is Habard to think of," said Ann, twisting a piece of silk round and round in her thin fingers.

"But you said . . . we finally agreed that he had only been philandering."

Ann looked out at the gray autumn sky and the clouds of scarlet and gold leaves hopping and tumbling across the lawns. "Well . . ." she said hesitantly. "It appears that he *should* marry you."

"Marry? What can you mean?"

"It is put about that his mama was *not* in residence and that you were alone together at Mullford Hall."

"Is there no end to all this spite and malice?" said Lucy. "Not only was his mother very much in residence but most of his relatives."

"But the Duchess is saying herself that he sent them all packing and that she herself went off on a visit the last two days, leaving

161

you alone together."

Ann watched as Lucy's face turned scarlet. Lucy was remembering how glad she had been when the Duchess had not joined them for dinner and how she had assumed that Her Grace was sulking in her room, having her meals from a tray.

"But Simon would never . . . he would have told me!" she said.

"Are you sure?"

"He is a *gentleman!*" said Lucy hotly.

"A gentleman who has not been near you since Guy's death," said Ann, picking up her sewing and stabbing a needle into the brocade.

"But how could he?" said Lucy reasonably. "There were ugly rumors. We were both being accused of the murder. To have been seen together at all would have been folly."

"But he could have written to you."

Lucy gave a little sigh and echoed sadly, "Yes, he could have written to me."

"Well, either his mama is lying, which from all accounts is a thing she does quite often, or you are compromised. But one way or t'other, the world believes you to have been compromised and Habard is expected to make an offer when your period of mourning is over."

"I cannot marry him."

"I thought you cared for him."

"Oh, I did," said Lucy. "But perhaps I was mistaken and besides you are probably right. He was probably only amusing himself. It's all my fault. I wanted to make Guy jealous and I asked Simon to be my lover."

"You *what?*"

"Well, you suggested . . ."

"Oh, my wretched tongue. This is dreadful."

"I did not sleep with him," said Lucy in a low voice. "He . . . he kept suggesting I try to repair my marriage . . . even when I threw myself at him."

Ann's thin face registered every degree of surprise.

"I think the man must have been in love with you after all," she said at last.

But Lucy shook her head. "There were times," she sighed, "when I began to think his feelings might be deeply touched. But I was there and I was available. That is all. I shall not see him again."

"Fiddle," said Ann briskly. "You cannot molder here in the country forever. Come back to Town with us for a few weeks."

"I am quite happy here," said Lucy. "I have so much work to do, it stops me from . . . thinking."

Lucy suddenly felt she had to get away from her friend. She wanted to be alone to think.

"I feel very hot indoors," said Lucy, rising to her feet. "I think I shall go for a walk on the grounds."

Ann opened her mouth to point out that the room was in fact becoming very chilly but she saw the distress in Lucy's eyes and contented herself by saying instead, "I shall not accompany you, Lucy dear. Giles is to join me presently."

Lucy walked out of the house into the flying wind under the flying clouds. The cloak she was wearing was the one she had worn when he had walked with her in the gardens.

Then she remembered the intensity in his voice when he had held the swing and said, "You enchant me."

But Lucy could not believe he loved her. The Marquess had taken away from her all self-esteem. She no longer saw a pretty girl when she looked in the glass but an insipid and colorless blond.

The blast from a horn blown on the wind from the direction of the south lodge made her frown.

Visitors.

For once, she was going to hide and leave Ann to do the entertaining.

She hid behind the wide, dark green skirts of a cedar and watched.

A muddy traveling carriage flanked by outriders appeared at a bend in the drive.

Seated on the box with his coachman beside him, his long hands holding the reins, was the Duke of Habard.

Lucy stepped out from the shelter of the trees.

His head jerked around and he reined in his team and then sat for a few moments looking down at the reins in his hands.

Then he gave instructions to the coachman who took his place and he jumped lightly down.

He was dressed in a scarlet garrick redingote with a top hat with vertical sides and a narrow brim set to a nicety on his crisp black hair.

He was more handsome than she had remembered, and more formidable.

"Lady Standish," he said, making her a low bow. "I present my compliments and also my condolences over your bereavement."

"Thank you," said Lucy faintly.

He surveyed her in silence and Lucy felt constrained to speak.

"Did you . . . have you come to stay with us, Your Grace? I did not receive your letter."

"I came without writing first," he answered. "Pray forgive me. I have a certain business matter to discuss with you. If my stay will inconvenience you, I can put up at the inn at Standish."

"No, Your Grace, we have plenty of bedchambers. Mr. and Mrs. Hartford are in residence and they will be delighted to see you." *Why are we so formal?* thought Lucy wildly. *Is this the man who kissed me so passionately?* "If you would care to accompany me to the house. . ." she began.

"No," he said, "I think not. What I have to say to you is better said in private."

"As you will," replied Lucy nervously,

looking around. "There is a summer house over by the lake, a gazebo, out of the wind."

She turned and led the way across the shaggy autumn lawns, through the swirling clouds of colored leaves, her blue coat billowing about her slight figure.

"And how are things in Town, Your Grace?" she asked, determined to be as formal as he.

"Very bad."

"The economy?"

"No. The scandal. It is that I wish to discuss with you."

"Oh," said Lucy ineffectually. The wind was ruffling the waters of the lake. A mallard duck bobbed past and disappeared among the reeds.

The gazebo was perched on a little knoll beside the lake. The wind whistled eerily though the criss-cross latticed slats over the windows like a dirge for summer past.

He indicated one of the stone seats and then sat next to her, arranging the skirts of his coat.

His face looked harsh and set and two grooves she had not noticed before ran down either side of his mouth. His eyes were hooded by their drooping lids. He slowly drew off his gloves, turning the soft leather this way and that in his long fingers.

"Has Mrs. Hartford said anything to you about London's latest scandal?" he said.

Lucy blushed painfully. "She said your mama was putting it about that she was not in residence when we . . . when we were together."

"Exactly. I made her deny the rumor, which she did by weeping and saying pathetically to her court of spongers, 'Simon has *commanded* me to say that I was present.' She was, in fact, there, you know, sulking in her rooms."

"Well . . . that was all very long ago," said Lucy, and it did seem to belong to another sunny world, far away on the other side of the black pit of her husband's death.

"But the gossip is very present," he said. "I do not care for myself. But you are very young and should not have your life blighted so."

"I do not plan to return to London," said Lucy, looking unseeingly out at the water, "so what society says about me need not affect me."

"That is the way you feel now," he said, "but that feeling will not last forever. Marry me."

"What?"

"I am asking you to marry me."

"Guy asked me, just as he was dying, not to marry again. He said he loved me. I gave him my promise."

"Selfish unto death," said the Duke coldly. "Do you know why I did not come near you? Because there were already ugly stories about that we had conspired to have your husband killed. Did you think me unfeeling and callous?"

"Yes."

"Did you think perhaps *I* had killed Guy?"

Lucy looked down at her shoes and said nothing.

"I see that you did. Never has my character been more maligned. I assure you, it will be the sensible thing to marry me."

"It would be shocking . . . so shocking, so soon after Guy's death."

"It is months since Guy's death. A year is not yet up. I suggest we become unofficially engaged."

"And this is the *business* proposition you mentioned earlier?"

"Yes."

"I have already been married once through a business proposition. I do not care for another."

"I see," he said in a low voice. "I thought it would be thus."

"Thought *what* would be thus?" said Lucy crossly. Oh, why didn't he take her in his arms? Why did he sit there, so aloof, so elegant? Had he never cared for her? Obviously not.

"I feel you really cared for your husband deeply."

"Oh," said Lucy, looking away. Well, her pride was not going to let her correct him. If marriage to her was only to be in the nature of a business proposition, then she wanted none of it.

She arose and shook out her skirts.

"I must refuse your kind offer," she said coldly. "But you are welcome to stay as my guest. The Hartfords will be delighted to see you again. Our cook does fairly well but not quite in the grand manner of a French chef. . . ."

She led the way out of the gazebo, talking lightly all the while, without ever looking back to see if he were following her or if he had accepted her invitation.

Chapter Eight

The Duke had elected to stay and had retired to the rooms allotted to him. Lucy found herself relieved to find that the Hartfords had gone to the village. She felt she could not bear to face Ann's questioning and hopeful eyes.

Her husband's effects, desk, and papers had been put away in an unused servant's room at the top of the house. Lucy had not looked at any of his belongings, but all at once she was overcome by a desire to search for evidence of his infidelity. To search for anything that would remove the guilt engendered by his last words.

The room smelt damp and musty and unaired. The papers which had been strewn about his study when it had been ransacked had all been collected into neat piles and placed on top of the desk.

The steward had gone through them to take away any outstanding bills and deal with them. Lucy's face suddenly went hot at the idea of the steward having come across the sort of evidence she herself was looking for.

She pulled up a hard kitchen chair, sat down in front of the desk, and lit a candle, for the day was growing dark as black clouds massed in the sky above.

The papers were mostly letters from friends

discussing arrangements to meet at prize fights or cock fights or coffeehouses.

There were no letters from women. Lucy discovered this after more than an hour of diligent reading.

Perhaps, she thought, she should have looked through bank letters and bills before the steward took them away. Although he had given the diamond earrings and pendant to Harriet, he had bought them for her, but the bills might have revealed evidence of other trinkets.

The desk was a tambour-fronted bureau, its top rolled back to reveal the flat top of the desk with its little pigeon-holes and drawers. She pulled open drawer after drawer in front of her, having already searched the larger ones below the desk top.

But all the papers seemed to have been removed and laid on top. One of the small drawers would not open. Feeling sure there would be nothing in it either, she somehow felt impelled to force it just to see.

She picked up a chisel-ended poker from the hearth and carefully inserted it under the drawer and yanked it up. There was a sharp splitting sound as the front of the drawer came away completely and fell in two pieces in front of her.

"Now I have ruined a perfectly good desk for nothing," mourned Lucy. The drawer was empty and she was about to rise when she sensed rather than saw a cavity at the back.

She held a candle up to the drawer and saw there was indeed a secret space at the back of the desk. She thrust her hand in and with a gasp of triumph felt a thick bundle of paper, which she pulled out.

Poor Lucy found herself looking down at all the evidence of her husband's infidelity that she could possibly require. There were letters from Harriet Comfort, and not only from her but from various other ladies of the *demimonde* who seemed delighted to flatter her late husband by praising, in quite startling detail, his prowess between the sheets.

She thrust the letters away from her finally, in disgust, and, as she did so, a small thick diary fell to the floor. She picked it up and turned the pages, looking curiously at the neat rows of figures. At the end of the book, in front of the last section, the Marquess had written, "If I should die, this is of Nashinul importance."

He never could spell, thought Lucy ruefully, tucking the diary into a pocket in her apron to study it more carefully later. Then she took the pile of love letters, put them in the fireplace, and then thrust the candle through the bars, watching them turn brown, curl up, and finally catch fire.

If only Simon loved me, thought Lucy sadly, *then I should accept him on the spot, for these letters have proved that Guy was never faithful to me. In fact it seems he began being unfaithful to me from the day we married.*

But there was nothing else to do except pray to get through the evening ahead with a modicum of dignity.

It was better than she expected. Ann and her husband were delighted to share the dinner table with the Duke of Habard and talked so gaily that they failed to notice that the elegant Duke was somewhat more somber than usual.

He looked heartbreakingly handsome, thought Lucy. His evening clothes were perfection, and only his eyes were as hard and cold as the diamonds in his stock and on his fingers.

"I have been wondering about Standish," he suddenly said when Ann paused for breath. "I cannot believe that his death was the result of some footpad's greed. If he had been stabbed or bludgeoned, it would seem more likely. But footpads do not normally shoot people, nor do they frequent the fashionable squares of the West End as much as they used to. There are very nasty rumors about Barrington. And Standish was involved with Barrington. Sir Percival Burke became very bosky at White's and started to mutter sinister remarks about Barrington having power over him. The next day, Sir Percival was found floating down the Thames."

"Oh, the bill broker fellow," said Giles Hartford comfortably. "Well, he's not sinister, you know. He fleeces young men of their lands and property, but so do all the other bill brokers

173

and money lenders, not to mention the gaming hells. Ain't anything sinister about that. Just sad."

"I have heard that Barrington craves power and a peerage or a knighthood, at the very least," said Habard as if Giles had not spoken.

He turned to Lucy and spoke to her directly for the first time since he had proposed to her in the gazebo.

"Did Standish say anything . . . or leave anything in his papers that might . . . ?"

"Oh, a most *odd* thing," cried Lucy, suddenly remembering the diary. "Wait!"

She ran from the room and Ann watched the way the Duke's eyes followed her retreating figure.

In a short time Lucy was back, the diary in her hand. "Only see," she said, bending over the Duke's chair with the diary. "Where he wrote that bit about his death and it being of national importance."

Ann noticed with wry amusement that in her excitement Lucy was leaning over the Duke, pressed against his shoulder, and that a faint flush was mounting to the Duke's cheeks.

Lucy was dressed in severe mourning but the black enhanced her fair looks, and the little lace cap, which she had donned in the hope that the Duke would realize she had joined the ranks of the dowagers, had slipped slightly to one side and gave her a frivolous, coquettish appearance.

"It is some form of code," said the Duke slowly. "It's probably very simple. The numbers represent the different letters of the alphabet. Let me see."

"Oh, we cannot possibly leave you gentlemen to your wine with all this excitement," said Ann. "Let us all retire to the drawing room and find pencils and papers. This is the best party game ever."

But try as they would, the numbers did not correspond to the letters of the alphabet. D, for example, should have corresponded with 4, but it did not.

The Duke tapped his pencil thoughtfully against his teeth. "There must be something important here," he said. "Perhaps he had a favorite book?"

Lucy shook her head. "Guy never read anything. I do not think he had been very well educated."

"Do you mind if I take this back to London with me when I leave tomorrow?" asked the Duke.

"No, of course not," said Lucy, feeling sad. She had hoped somehow that he would have decided to stay a little longer. On the other hand, he did not love her. Only witness how courteously aloof his behavior had been since he arrived.

"I think we should retire, Giles," said Ann suddenly.

"Eh, what? Night's young, m'dear."

"And I'm *tired*," said Ann, giving him a loaded look and jerking her head in the direction of the Duke and Lucy.

"Oh, what? Eh? Oh, *I* see. Well, of course, I'm tired myself. You will excuse us, Lucy, Habard?"

Lucy flushed delicately. "Since His Grace is leaving us tomorrow, perhaps we should all retire?"

"I did not say anything about leaving early," murmured the Duke, his eyes on the thick diary in his hands.

Ann whipped her smiling and chuckling husband out of the room and Lucy looked at the Duke rather helplessly. If he did not care for her and only wanted to marry her because of a lot of malicious gossips, then she wished to be shot of him.

But he had once kissed her so passionately. Men, on the other hand, had mysterious lusts which women were supposed to tolerate, but not understand. Lucy raised her little hand to her suddenly hot face. Perhaps she had been rationalizing love into lust.

The Duke looked up suddenly and studied her flushed face.

"What are you thinking?" he asked abruptly.

"I was thinking about lust," said Lucy, and then blushed so hard she felt as if she had been dipped in boiling water.

He looked at her thoughtfully and then stretched out his long legs and leaned his head back against the wing of the chair.

"About whose lust, I wonder?" he murmured. "Yours or mine?"

Lucy made an embarrassed little movement with her hands. "My unruly tongue," she said wretchedly. "I was merely considering the difference between men and women."

"When it comes to lust, there is no difference," he said.

"But love . . . ?"

"Ah, love. What is your definition of love, Lucy?"

"Oh, caring for someone," she said slowly. "Feeling comfortable when they are there, and . . . and unhappy when they are not."

A log shifted and fell in the grate. The wind howled in the chimney and another fire-castle crumbled into ruins.

"And that is how you felt about your husband?"

"Yes, no . . . I don't remember."

"Do you feel comfortable when I am present?"

"Ah, no."

"Why?"

"I do not know. You make me feel . . . awkward."

His face suddenly was lit with that characteristically sweet smile of his and she felt her legs beginning to tremble.

"Lucy," he said gently, studying her from under his heavy lids as he leaned his head against the worn gold brocade of the chair, "do you not feel what lies in this room between us at the moment? It is there, humming and throbbing. I was worried, you see, that all feeling was on my side. But your breast is rising and falling in such a delectable way, and there is a treacherous little blue vein beating at the base of your neck. . . ."

"It is the heat," said Lucy, studying the floor. "The fire is very hot, you see."

"Yes. Very hot."

"And . . . and I think we should retire. . . ."

"By all means."

She stood up suddenly, looking down at him in quick disappointment. She had thought he meant . . . oh, she did not know what she hoped for.

She crossed the room and stood beside his chair, looking down at him. He raised his eyes and looked full into hers, something in the back of his silver gaze holding her trapped.

He slowly held out his hand, palm upwards.

"Then take my hand, Lucy," he said gently, "and say goodnight."

Lucy slowly put her hand into his, feeling the strength of his long fingers as his hand closed over her own. A fire seemed to run up her arm and course through her body. Helpless, buffeted by strong emotion, she looked down at him, a glint of tears shining in her eyes.

"If our joined hands can cause such tumult, Lucy," he said huskily, "only think, my sweeting, the delights of our joined bodies."

Lucy suddenly thought of her yearning sweetness during her courtship with Guy, followed by the thrashing, tumbling disillusionment of the marriage bed. She looked at him sadly, her high color fading and leaving her very pale.

"You should not talk to me thus, Your Grace," she said primly. She tugged her hand free and marched to the door, her head held high.

She put her hand on the knob and then slowly turned and looked at him. He had risen to his feet and was standing with his hands on his hips, his eyes narrowed in thought.

"I have it!" he said, his face clearing. "It is all very simple. What a fool I am!"

"What?"

"I love you, you silly widgeon. I have not been in love before and I am not in the way of saying it. I also have my pride and did not want to wish a rebuff and so proposed marriage on a business footing. But one of us must be brave. So here is my love, Lucy, and my heart, and my soul with it. Will you take it?"

"Oh, *yes,* Simon," gulped Lucy, rushing into his arms with such force that she nearly knocked him over. "Oh, *yes.*"

His arms closed about her like steel bands as his mouth descended on hers. He kissed her long and hard until they both were shaking. Lucy's fair hair was tumbled about her shoulders and the fichu she had modestly knotted over the low bosom of her dress had been sent flying across the room.

Exploring hands, restless hands, demanding, possessive mouth that moved so bewitchingly over and in her own, senses screaming for fulfillment . . . and yet when he murmured, "A more comfortable place to continue, I think," she went rigid in his arms, all the conventions crying out that it was a sin to lie with him without the blessing of the church.

He gave a little sigh and put her from him, looking down at her with a tender, amused smile. "We will just have to marry in secret, and very soon — as soon as possible. Then when your year of mourning is over, we will be married again with great pomp and circumstance."

"I'm sorry. You must think me a prude," mumbled Lucy, putting her arms around his neck and burying her face in his shirt frill.

"I think you a darling." He smiled. "I must go to London tomorrow. There are certain matters in Town that demand my attention. Will you come with me?"

"Ann and Giles have asked me to spend some time with them," said Lucy shyly. "I could follow you in about . . . oh . . . two days' time."

"Very well. I will take the mysterious diary with me. Now, kiss me goodnight, Lucy. The Courtlands are giving a ball. Remember, I first saw you at their house? I will meet you there . . .

on Thursday. Oh, Lucy, I love you so very much. . . ."

It was a merry party that set out for London two days later. Ludy was aglow with love and Ann and Giles were delighted with their young friend's happiness.

Lucy had made a tender farewell to the Duke the morning after she had accepted his proposal of marriage. It was wonderful to know that she would be seeing him again so soon, wonderful to think of walking into the Courtlands' ballroom and seeing him, waiting there.

The day before their own departure had been marred by an unexpected visit from Mr. Jerry Carruthers. He had claimed a close friendship with Guy and had said that Guy had kept certain letters and papers which he now wished to reclaim.

As the carriage jogged and rattled on its way to London and Ann and Giles both fell asleep, Lucy found herself puzzling more and more over Mr. Carruthers's strange visit.

Mr. Carruthers was a big, burly young man who affected the worst of the Corinthian style. He wore a belcher neckerchief knotted around his throat in place of a cravat and had many whip points stuck in his lapel. His leather breeches and riding boots had been spattered with mud when he had arrived, and yet he seemed to take pride in sitting down to luncheon in his dirt. He ogled Lucy quite dreadfully and paid her a great deal of overwarm compliments until Ann Hartford had called him to heel with a sharp remark, begging him to remember his hostess was a widow.

Immediately all fawning solicitation, Mr. Carruthers had begun to tell a great many sentimental stories concerning his great friendship with the late Marquess, which had all rung false.

Lucy could only be glad that she had burned all Guy's love letters, for she had at last to give in and allow Mr. Carruthers permission to search Guy's desk. He had eventually appeared downstairs looking . . . *relieved,* yes, relieved was the word for it, thought Lucy. He had immediately announced his intention of departing.

As he stood in the hall, making his adieux, he had said, "Well, I must have been mistaken, or Guy must have burned my papers. He certainly left nothing incriminating." And "incriminating" had been a strange word to use.

"Unless, of course," Giles Hartford had said jovially, "all that nonsense about what Guy knew being of national importance means anything."

Lucy frowned. That was when Mr. Jerry Carruthers had rounded on her, loomed over her, his eyes hard and bright, and demanded, "What is it? What is he talking about?"

Why Lucy had all at once decided to lie, she did not know. But she had flashed Giles a

182

warning glance and had said lightly, "Oh, Mr. Hartford was funning."

"You are sure?" Mr. Carruthers's face was very close to her own and he had grasped her arm.

"Yes, indeed," Lucy had snapped. "You were just leaving, Mr. Carruthers."

And so he left, looking over his shoulder at her all the while. There was something about his stare, something about the sinister hunch of his shoulders, that caused Lucy to call out lightly, "You need not look so, Mr. Carruthers. Mr. Hartford was in jest."

"Look like what?" he demanded, one hand on the pommel of his saddle, ready to mount.

"Why!" laughed Lucy. "Like the first murderer."

And that was when Mr. Carruthers had muttered, *"You know,"* and then he had flung himself into the saddle and had ridden away.

It was all very strange, thought Lucy wearily. No doubt Simon would decipher Guy's diary, and find that what the late Marquess had considered of national importance was the measurement of Miss Harriet Comfort's left ankle.

She shrugged. Mr. Carruthers was part of the past, part of a boorish section of London society she wished to forget. The swaying and jolting of the carriage soon lulled her and very soon she was asleep.

They stopped at a posting house for the

night, Ann and Giles electing to retire early so that they could proceed with their journey at first light in the morning.

But Lucy could not sleep. She was overcome with a longing to see Simon again, overcome, at the same time, with a strange dread that somehow she would not.

Her maid had contracted a severe chill a few days before and so Lucy had decided to do without the services of a maid until the woman was well again. She was about to rise from her seat by the bedroom fire and prepare for bed when there came a scratching at the door.

Lucy opened it to reveal the landlord. "There's a gentleman below, my lady," he said, handing her a card with one corner turned down.

Lucy held up the bed candle and read the inscription, "Mr. Jerry Carruthers."

She bit her lip. "Tell Mr. Carruthers I am retired for the night," she said.

"I dunno he'll listen, my lady," said the landlord. "Said it was urgent."

"Oh, very well," said Lucy crossly. She swung her cloak about her shoulders and followed the thick-set figure of the landlord downstairs.

Mr. Carruthers was waiting in the small hallway. His eyes flickered strangely in the candlelight as he watched her descend.

"I am so sorry to inconvenience you, Lady Standish," he said smoothly.

"Well, it *is* rather late, Mr. Carruthers. How

on earth did you know I was resident at this inn?"

"I had to see you," he said, ignoring her question.

He was dressed very plainly and formally in black coat and knee breeches. His hair was powdered and he looked more like a country parson dressed in his best than the swarthy Corinthian of a few days ago. Furthermore, he was wearing a small pair of steel spectacles, behind which his black eyes looked blacker and more fathomless than usual.

"I have news of your husband," he said rather breathlessly.

Lucy paled. "I think you are a little elated, Mr. Carruthers. May I remind you my husband is dead."

"Oh, I know," he said impatiently. "It is staggering news about something he found out. Why he was killed."

"Then tell me," snapped Lucy.

"I can't . . . not here. It is too public. If you could step into my carriage for a moment . . . it is in the inn yard."

Lucy hesitated. The need, however, to find any scrap of news that might clear her name, might clear Simon's name, was tempting.

A noisy burst of laughter came from the tap.

"See," he said eagerly. "Anyone might hear us. Come. It will only take a minute."

"Very well," said Lucy, drawing her cloak tightly about her shoulders.

Outside, the night air was bitter cold. A small moon gave hardly any light at all. Hoar frost glittered on the cobbles of the inn yard.

"Your carriage, sir?" demanded Lucy.

"My silly man must have left it on the road," replied Mr. Carruthers, putting a hand under her arm and urging her forward.

Just outside the inn yard, a light traveling carriage was standing under the black shadow of a stand of trees. The blinds were down and the carriage lamps were unlit.

Lucy suddenly knew that something was very wrong. She turned and looked towards the inn and then back again at the carriage.

"No, Mr. Carruthers," she began firmly. "I think I will return to —"

But that was as far as she got. A savage blow struck her behind the ear and she tumbled forward unconscious on the ground.

Jerry Carruthers put the small bludgeon that had felled her back in his coat pocket and stooped and picked up her light body with ease.

He carried it to the carriage, jerked open the door, and tumbled the unconscious body onto the floor inside. Stooping over Lucy, he quickly gagged and bound her.

Then he hurried back to the inn.

The landlord listened gravely as he explained that Lady Standish was leaving to make an urgent call on a sick friend in the neighborhood. Should her friends ask for her, this is what they were to be told. But if they did not, why, there was no point in waking them.

"And what name shall I say, sir?" asked the landlord. "I took your card to her ladyship but I don't recall the name."

Jerry, who had already hoped that the landlord could not read, smiled and said, "Parsons. The Reverend Parsons."

"Very good, Mr. Parsons," said the landlord. "I'll tell Mr. and Mrs. Hartford, should they be asking."

Jerry Carruthers bowed and walked back out of the inn, thinking furiously.

He had told Barrington long before that he was afraid the Marchioness of Standish might find some evidence among her husband's papers that would implicate him in the murder of the Prime Minister, not to mention Sir Percival Burke and the Marquess of Standish. Barrington had given his orders. If Lady Standish showed any signs of suspicion, then she must be killed.

Now she had, but kill her he could not. Mr. Carruthers found, somewhat to his amazement, that he could not kill a woman. He had already explained as much to Barrington after his headlong flight from Standish, and so Barrington had smiled and given his instructions. Lady Standish was to be taken to Li, Li would dispose of both Lady Standish and her remains, and then they could be comfortable again.

But Mr. Carruthers finally knew that the suspicions would never end. Barrington was mad. Barrington had gone slowly mad after Erskine had not been elected as Prime Minister and so all hopes of a peerage had gone.

But Barrington was sane enough to realize he still held Jerry Carruthers in his power. Jerry thought of his wife and how she would react if certain information and letters reached her.

He shuddered more over that thought than he did over the idea that Barrington would surely find a way to turn him over to the authorities for the murder of the Prime Minister if he did not carry out his orders.

By the time he had left Lucy's still-unconscious body with Li, the leaden dawn was streaking over London and a few flakes of snow were whipping though a biting, howling wind.

Mr. Barrington lived in a crumbling house on the Surryside, set a little apart from the huddle of tenements which crouched around it by a half-acre of weedy garden.

Again, Mr. Carruthers was amazed at the insanity of the man who had hoped to become a lord and yet who elected to live in such squalid surroundings as these.

Mr. Barrington himself answered the door. He had lost weight and his clothes hung on his body; drooping pendulous pouches of flabby skin swung on either side of his pursed mouth.

But the usual joviality was there, albeit this time mad and hectic.

"Well, is the deed done?" asked Mr.

Barrington. He stumbled ahead, up the creaking stairs as the rising wind tore at the old building.

"Yes," said Mr. Carruthers curtly. "Li will see to the rest."

"Good, good, we will have a drink." Mr. Barrington pushed open a door on the first landing and led the way into a parlor, unfurnished except for a deal table and two rickety chairs.

He poured out two measures of gin from a green bottle into thick, greasy tumblers and stood with his back to the window, blocking out most of the light.

"Your health," he said, raising his glass.

Mr. Carruthers grunted and tossed the spirits down his throat. The whole house seemed to shudder and heave in the gale, for all the world like a prison hulk.

"What a place to live," said Carruthers. "I would have thought that with your social ambitions, you would have set up house in the West End."

"I was not prepared to sport my blunt until the peerage was a fact," said Mr. Barrington with a sort of mad amiability.

"It's a wonder you didn't try to get your claws into one of the Prince Regent's friends," said Mr. Carruthers curiously. "That way your peerage would have been assured."

"I could have got it through Erskine," replied his host. "Why wasn't Erskine elected? All my plots and plans gone for nothing, not to mention a fortune in getting a deal of silly, useless young men like yourself in my power."

"I have killed three men on your behalf," said Mr. Carruthers hotly. "I do not call that the act of a weak man."

"And yet you could not kill a woman."

Jerry Carruthers helped himself to another tot of gin. "Killing," he sneered. "We'll never escape suspicion. You'll have to kill the whole of London."

"Not I," said Mr. Barrington equably as the house gave another shudder and heave. "You should have interrogated Lady Standish first. You should have found out whom she had talked to."

"I was simply carrying out orders," said Mr. Carruthers sulkily. "Li's probably disposed of her by now."

"Yes, a good girl is Li," said Mr. Barrington, as if praising a serving maid.

"Why should I care?" muttered Mr. Carruthers, drinking more gin. "Human life is cheap in this horrible city. People kill each other every minute of the day. What's a few more lives?"

Mr. Barrington sat down on the chair opposite and tilted the green bottle, watching the liquor rise in his glass. "Frightened of divine retribution?" he asked.

"Don't start that," said Mr. Carruthers wrathfully. "If anyone's going to rot in hell, 'tis you!"

"You are too nervous, my friend," Mr. Barrington smiled. "No one will find out about us . . . ever."

"That Giles Hartford was saying something about Guy finding out something of national importance."

"Then he must be killed too."

"He must . . . let me out of here!" Jerry Carruthers leapt to his feet, knocking the chair over. "You're *mad*. I'm mad. We're all mad. I should kill you and do the world a favor."

"You forget, I hold papers of yours which will be published on the event of my untimely death."

Mr. Carruthers turned and sat down at the table again, after righting the chair. He calmly helped himself to more gin, and grinned at Mr. Barrington over the rim of his glass.

"A thought has suddenly come to me," he said. "You have closed shop in Fetter Lane. You've closed your business. You're too clutch-fisted to pay a lawyer to hold papers when you ain't in business, see? Therefore, my friend, I think you have all the papers in this rathole of a house!"

"I would not be so stupid," said Barrington, his eyes moving restlessly about the room.

"We'll see," said Mr. Carruthers. He took a pistol from his pocket and began to prime it. "Now, you may sit there like the horrible old codger you are, and don't try to stop me."

Mr. Barrington looked down at the oily remains of his gin and did not look up.

Triumphantly, Jerry Carruthers left the room. He ran through the creaking, shaking house as great gusts of snow billowed past the dirty windows.

It was deathly cold, and every room was filled with the beating sound of the storm.

He searched through the moldering rooms, full of old furniture and bric-a-brac, and through the empty cellars. He at last found what he was searching for as he pushed open the door of an attic at the top of the house.

Papers and documents were piled up on shelves, mountains and mountains of paper. "It will take a year to find mine," he muttered savagely. Up at the top of the house, the noise of the storm was immense. The whole building shuddered and creaked and groaned.

He saw a stub of a candle on the mantelpiece and lit it with a lucifer. Then he ran about the room, setting pile after pile of papers alight.

"Free," he muttered as the papers started to blaze. "Now to get out of here."

He wrenched at the door and found it locked.

"The old fox." He grinned. "That will not stay me for long."

He took out his pistol and shot the lock clear away, and then pushed confidently at the door. To his horror, it refused to budge. A low chuckle came from the other side, and then the sound of heavy objects being piled on the other side of the door.

"Let me out!" he screamed.

Somewhere over the racket of the storm came the sound of a laugh.

He turned desperately and faced the flaming inferno of the room. There was only one window and it was barred. His clothes caught fire and he screamed and beat at the flames with his hands.

There was a tremendous crack of wind. The building seemed to rear up like a horse, and then slowly it started to tumble in and collapse like a house of cards. Flames and plaster and dust rose into the blinding sheets of snow.

Jerry Carruthers inside the blazing room and Mr. Barrington outside — both plunged to their deaths through the splitting, collapsing floors.

No one came to help. The storm was too severe. People died in London all the time in the ruins of falling buildings. One or two more bodies was not an out-of-the-way thing, after all.

Mr. Barrington would have appreciated that philosophy.

Had he been alive, of course.

Chapter Nine

Lucy, Marchioness of Standish, lay still and listened to the storm, frozen with fear. Her gag had been removed although her wrists were still bound behind her back. She was too frightened to utter a sound.

The main focus of her fear was the other occupant of the room — the strange silent figure in the grotesque, glittering robes, the white-painted face, and the almond eyes — who sat on a low couch at the other end, as unmoving as a statue.

The narrow room was bathed in white light from the snow outside. How long had she been unconscious, wondered Lucy — a day? A year?

At last the still figure of Li moved. She searched in her robes and took out a long, wicked knife, and advanced on Lucy.

Lucy opened her mouth to scream but no sound came out.

She struggled into a sitting position and watched the approaching knife, hypnotized. Then she noticed that Li was carrying a length of clothesline in her other hand. The Chinese girl stooped over her, and Lucy shut her eyes. To her surprise, she felt the bonds of her wrists being cut and then one end of the clothesline was tied firmly round her ankles. Li tottered across the room on her bound feet, and fastened the other end onto an iron ring on the wall. She turned and surveyed Lucy thoughtfully, turning the long knife over in her beringed fingers, and then, with an odd little bow, she left the room.

It seemed to Lucy as if death were inevitable. She would never see Simon again. With all absence of hope, a blessed numbness crept over her mind and body and she sat unmoving on the floor.

The door opened again, and Li came in bearing a tray on which was a bottle of wine, a glass, a quartern loaf, and a lump of cheese.

She put the food on the floor next to Lucy and then retired to the couch, where she sat down with her legs tucked up under her robes, and surveyed her prisoner with an unblinking stare.

Lucy looked at the food and looked at Li and looked at the food again. After some hesitation, she helped herself to some wine, and then realized she was ravenously hungry. The street sounds which she had noticed when she had recovered consciousness had rapidly faded as the storm outside grew in intensity. There was a small fire burning in the grate, and she shakily stretched out her hands to the blaze.

"Bleedin' cold, innit?" said the Chinese vision suddenly.

At the sound of that Cockney voice, hope flooded Lucy's chilled body. But Li looked as strange, as alien, and as unwinking as ever, and with a little sigh, Lucy thought she must be imagining things.

"I don't like it. Not a bit!" Li spoke again and Lucy gave a nervous start.

"You speak English?" she exclaimed.

"Yus," said Li moodily. "I *am* English, ain't I? But the way some goes on, you'd think I come out o' 'ell. Stick 'er in the ribs, 'e says, says 'e. Nuthin' to the likes of you. But I got feelings," said Li passionately. "If we wus to 'ave a bit o' a fight, that's different, but just stickin' someone, ain't my ken."

"Oh, don't kill me!" cried Lucy. "I will pay you. Please don't kill me. Why should you? Who wants me dead?"

"I can't tell you," said Li. "But I took the money, din't I? So I gots to do it some'ow."

"But I will pay you *more*," cried Lucy desperately, while a kaleidoscope of colored thoughts tumbled through her head. *Simon, if only I can see you again . . . oh, Mother and Father, no more will I keep you in social seclusion . . . could I overpower this girl and get the knife away from her?*

Li surveyed her thoughtfully. "Temptin'," she said after a pause. "Very temptin'. But they'd kill me an I wouldn't stay alive long enuff to enjoy it. Who are you, anways?"

"My name is Lucy, Marchioness of Standish."

" 'Ere! You're never."

"I assure you that I am, and if you get me out of here . . ."

But Li had stopped listening and had begun muttering to herself.

"That old fox, I knew 'e'd gone barmy. Every runner, every watch, every constable in the 'ole of London'll be arter me. Oh. Gawdstreuth!"

"Which old fox?" asked Lucy. And then with a sudden flash of intuition, she leaned forward. "Do you mean Mr. Barrington?"

Li shook her head slowly from side to side so that the fake jewels on her headdress glittered and sparkled. "Now you been and gone and done it," she said. "I got to kill you now. You knows too much."

With a sad little sigh she pulled the knife out from her robes.

Lucy jumped to her feet, straining at the halter that held her prisoner.

At that moment, there came a tremendous knocking at the door.

"Open up in there!" cried a man's voice over the sound of the wind.

"Simon!" screamed Lucy. "Simon! She's going to kill me!"

The door heaved on its hinges and crashed open as the Duke splintered the lock. Li rushed forward and held the knife to Lucy's throat.

"I'll kill 'er," she said fiercely, "if you take one step forward."

Lucy looked at the Duke with agonized eyes. A great deal of men seemed to be pushing into the low room behind him. In front of them was Harriet Comfort, white and shivering, a great bruise marking one side of her face.

"Li!" she screamed. "Barrington's dead."

For the first time, Li's impassive face showed expression. Her mouth dropped open and her eyebrows rose up under her headdress.

Then, quick as a flash, she dropped the knife and scampered into the far room, slamming and barring the door behind her before the surge of men, headed by the Duke, could reach her.

The Duke caught Lucy in his arms and held her close. "I never thought to see you alive again," he murmured. "Don't cry, Lucy, it's all over now."

There was a splintering crash as his servants broke down the door through which Li had fled. But of the Chinese girl, there was no sign. It turned out that holes had been knocked through the walls of the adjoining houses to supply the mostly criminal inmates of the street with a fast means of escape.

For the first time, Lucy began to feel really ill. Her head throbbed, and the room swung before her eyes. The Duke cut the rope that was tied around her waist and turned to take her in his arms again. And just in time. For with a little choked sob, Lucy fainted dead away.

Lucy was to be ill for a long time. One of the most severe winters London had known raged outside the Hartfords' home where she lay for weeks in the grips of a fever.

And then at last, when Ann Hartford was about to give up hope, the fever abated, leaving Lucy white and thin and weak.

She held onto Ann's hand and murmured, "Simon."

"Gone to the country," said Ann softly. "He has been here, every day and night, since you arrived. The minute your fever abated, he had to leave to see to his affairs. He will be back soon."

"How soon?" whispered Lucy hoarsely, her mind filled with all sorts of nameless perils which could stop his return.

"A few weeks," said Ann soothingly. "Plenty of time for you to recover your looks."

"A few *weeks*," Lucy said, struggling to raise herself up on the pillows. "And my looks! Give me a looking glass."

"The affairs of his estate were pressing," said Ann, pushing Lucy back with a firm hand. "And you will have a looking glass when you are feeling stronger."

"No! Now!"

"Very well." Ann silently handed her a glass.

"Oh, dear," said Lucy. "Is that really me?"

A thin, wasted face with huge, dark circles under the eyes stared back at her. Her hair hung lank and dull over her forehead.

"You have been very, very ill," said Ann quietly. "Now you will recover. And you must never doubt Habard's love. His devotion was . . . very moving."

"Tell me what happened . . . to Barrington?" asked Lucy.

"Later," said Ann, watching Lucy's eyelids beginning to droop. "It is a fantastic story. Your parents have called every day. You must be strong for them too."

But Lucy was already asleep.

In the days that followed, Lucy began to piece together bits and pieces of the story until she had nearly the whole.

The Duke had broken the code. He realized he had been trying too hard, and that whatever the code was, it was bound to be something simple. One could hardly consider the late Marquess an intellectual. And so he had counted from the end of the alphabet instead of the beginning, and there he had it.

The authorities were quickly alerted. At first, they could not find Barrington or Carruthers. The Marquess and Sir Percival Burke were dead. The Earl of Oxtead had fled the country and rumor had it he had been killed by Napoleon's troops in a drunken brawl.

Young Harry Chalmers had fought like a tiger before he was finally subdued. He at last admitted that Jerry Carruthers had been responsible for the deaths of the Marquess and Sir Percival, after he had disposed of the Prime Minister.

But apart from the address in Fetter Lane, he

did not know where else Barrington might be.

The Duke, his servants, and the authorities had searched all over London for the missing bill broker.

And then the Hartfords had arrived, terrified and exhausted with their story of the mysterious abduction of Lucy.

It was then that the Duke had thought to call on Harriet Comfort. What had transpired there, Ann said, no one knew, but he had managed to find Barrington's address. But when they got to Surrey-side, the house was a blazing ruin. They had dug frantically, the Duke crying Lucy's name, everyone convinced that her dead body would be found in the rubble. But only the bodies of Barrington and Carruthers had been found. And that was when the Duke had returned to Harriet Comfort's and had emerged, dragging her behind him.

"She knew nothing of the plot to kill the Prime Minister. But she did know where Li could be found. And so . . . the rest you know."

Lucy was out of bed and lying on a chaise longue in the Hartfords' drawing room as Ann finished the story.

"Simon does not say when he will return," said Lucy, looking out at the pale sunshine. "In fact, I am not quite sure *what* he says in his letters at all. It is amazing that such an elegant man should have such atrocious handwriting."

But Lucy would not admit to qualms of unease. She had been able to decipher most of Simon's letters and they had seemed very correct and formal, although he always showed concern for her health.

Ann told her she was vastly improved in looks, but Lucy had lost confidence. All the glass told her was that she looked pale and insignificant.

What if Simon had met some other lady? What if his letters showed that he really considered her only as a friend?

And so Lucy's worried thoughts twisted and turned in her head as the long winter passed and the days grew lighter and still he did not come.

She was now allowed visitors. Her parents came almost every day. Lucy found the courage to tell them she had lied about the court dress.

"Well!" gasped Mrs. Hyde-Benton. "It was very naughty of you, dear, but I suppose we must forgive our little puss now she is to marry a Duke."

"I have not seen him for some time," said Lucy. "Mayhap he will not be of the same mind."

"Never say so," cried her mother. "He is honor bound to marry you and so we shall tell him."

"Oh, *no*, Mama," said Lucy wretchedly. "Not another arranged marriage. I could not bear it. I want a man who loves me for myself."

"You are very unworldly," said her father severely. "You would not have married into the aristocracy in the first place had we not taken matters in hand."

"And you consider it a great thing that I was married to a criminal, a wastrel, and a womanizer?" said Lucy.

"You mustn't be so rigid, dear," said her mother. "The aristocracy will have their little ways. I hope you aren't going to be too prudish with His Grace. A fine thing it would be if you threw away this magnificent chance because of your moralizing. I don't know where you get it from."

"No, Mama," said Lucy quietly. What on earth would Simon think of these parents of hers? But she had resolved never to exclude them from her home or friends again. Guy had been wrong. But on the other hand . . . she had a sudden vision of the elegant and fastidious Duke entertaining her mother and father to dinner, and shuddered.

And then she felt ashamed of herself. Her parents loved her very much and had done their best for her as far as they could see it. It was no use pointing out that her marriage had nearly led to her death.

Furthermore, Simon's mother came from a low background and behaved disgracefully. But then society always forgave an outrageous, vulgar eccentric with a title while they looked askance at pushing, pretentious middle class.

But none of these worried thoughts appeared on Lucy's face, and she set herself to turn Mr.

and Mrs. Hyde-Benton's minds from the subject of the Duke of Habard.

After her parents had left, a late post brought a letter from Simon. She screwed up her eyes in an effort to decipher his scrawl. At last it emerged that he was due back in London shortly and looked forward to the pleasure of calling on her. It was simply signed "S" as usual, no words of love or affection.

Despite a sinking feeling that his feelings had definitely cooled towards her, Lucy spent the next days slaving to improve her appearance, and the house seemed filled from morning till night with couturieres, mantua makers, and hairdressers.

For the following two days, she sat waiting, perfumed and dressed, too nervous to even sew or read a book, jumping nervously every time carriage wheels sounded on the cobbles outside.

Matters were not helped by overhearing Ann muttering to Giles, "I could *kill* Habard. What ails the man? If he had changed in his affections, at least he could write and put her out of her misery."

And so the next day, Lucy brushed out the hairdresser's elaborate art and tied her hair back at the nap of her neck with a black silk ribbon. The weather had turned chilly again and so she put on a comfortable kerseymere wool dress and half-boots.

She picked up a novel and forced herself to

read until she became absorbed in the story. When a carriage rattled over the cobbles outside, she did not even look up.

Ann and Giles had left to visit relatives, and Lucy had given instructions to the servants that she was not to be disturbed.

All callers were to be firmly told that the Marchioness was not at home.

She did not raise her eyes from the page when the door opened, assuming it to be a footman with logs for the fire.

"Still in mourning, I see," said a dry voice.

Then her eyes flew up and she started to her feet, the book falling from her lap.

The Duke of Habard was standing framed in the doorway, handsome as ever, tall and elegant in impeccable morning dress from his sculptured cravat to his glossy hessians.

"No," said Lucy, "I am not in mourning. You see . . ." She wanted to tell him that she had given up hoping he would come — had put on old, comfortable clothes and that was why she was wearing a black ribbon in her hair and a gray dress — but somehow the words died on her lips.

"May I sit down?" he asked.

"Of course," said Lucy, while all the time her heart was crying out to him to take her in his arms and to kiss all her fears away.

But his eyes were cold and hard. He sat down on a hardback chair, took out a snuff box, and deftly took a pinch with an elegance which would have made even Lord Petersham stare with envy.

"I trust I find you recovered," said this stiff and formal stranger who sat in the Duke of Habard's clothes and had the Duke of Habard's voice.

"Yes," said Lucy faintly.

"I am much relieved," he said. "I was troubled about your health. You endured a great ordeal."

I want to ask him what happened, thought Lucy wildly. But I am afraid. Obviously, he not only does not love me, but he does not like me one little bit.

"You received my letters?" asked the Duke politely.

"Yes . . . yes, indeed," said Lucy faintly.

"Oh, you did," said the Duke with sudden savagery. "Amazing!"

"Amazing?" said Lucy, looking bewildered. "Are the posts so bad?"

"I see you are of a mind to be sarcastic," he said coldly.

To Lucy's horror, he got to his feet, indicating that the call was at an end.

"I am glad to see you are fully recovered in body, if not in mind," he said with a magnificent bow. "Let us hope your great grief will soon be overcome."

And with a smaller bow from the waist, he stalked towards the door.

In that moment, all breeding, all conventional training fell from Lucy's shaking shoulders, leaving a raw, hurting, rejected woman.

"So she's got her claws in you as well," she spat out in the direction of his retreating back. "So you called on her to find out the whereabouts of Li? And what exactly did you do?"

He swung round then, his eyes glittering. "Have you gone demented? Of whom are you talking?"

"Her!" screamed Lucy, jumping up and down with jealous rage. "Harriet Comfort."

"Harriet . . . ?" He strode across the room and took Lucy by the shoulders and shook her.

"How dare you couple my name with that of a doxy? Have I not stood enough? Was it not enough to learn that you are still wasting away with grief for that miserable husband of yours? To allow me to pour out my passion and love in all those letters and —"

"Stop!" said Lucy. "Oh, Simon. *What* are you talking about?"

"I paid a call on your parents before I came here," he said, glaring down at her, "to ask permission to pay my addresses. I was informed by both your parents that it was only to be expected of me after I . . . *I* — mark you — had caused such a scandal. I wished for a speedy wedding, but they counseled me to wait until you had recovered from your grief for Standish. I pointed out that you could not be grieving over the death of such a useless, weak, and criminal man, and your mother shook her head and smiled and said, 'Oh, poor, dear Guy. Such a wild, young man. Youth will have its follies.' "

"Oh, dear," said Lucy, going limp in his grasp. "Do not hold me so tightly, Simon, you are hurting me. My poor, silly parents. No, I do not grieve for Guy one little bit. I thought you had forgot me, that you no longer loved me."

"But my letters . . ."

"Of passion and love?" Lucy smiled. "Simon, *really.* I have them by me. I always keep your letters near me. Read one!"

She went over to a writing desk in the corner and selected a letter at random from the pile. The Duke quickly scanned it. "Your writing is very hard to decipher, Simon," said Lucy, "but you must admit your letters are very formal."

"Well, *this* one is. Let me see the others."

He quickly scanned three more, holding up his quizzing glass and staring at the parchment in increasing dismay.

"Strange," he murmured. "When I wrote to you, I felt all the feelings of love and passion and I was sure I was writing them down."

Lucy came to stand next to him. "If you will look in *that* one," she said smiling, "you will find a vastly passionate description of the prospective ploughing of the five acre."

He put the letter down and looked at her very seriously. "You do not care for me, Lucy?"

"I love you with all my heart."

He caught her in his arms and slowly bent his mouth to hers. Her eyelids closed, and her own mouth turned up to receive his kiss.

The storm of passion that shook both of them was worse than ever before. At last, he looked ruefully down at her swollen lips and murmured, "If we are going to wait, then I cannot bear much more of this. How could you ever think I would even look at Harriet Comfort after having held you in my arms?"

"She had a terrible bruise on her face," said Lucy.

"It was necessary to beat some of the information out of her," he said. "I had little time."

"Oh," said Lucy, looking up at him doubtfully. "Would you beat me, Simon?"

"If you tried to leave me, yes."

"Kiss me again, Simon."

"Yes . . . no. Not here."

"Where?"

"In my bed."

"But *Simon* . . ."

"Now. Come with me now before the Hartfords return. You have no idea what hell I suffered, thinking you were dead, thinking you were lost to me. Is it too shocking an idea? Lucy, look at me? My waistcoat knows your answer but I cannot hear it."

Lucy shyly raised her head.

"Yes, Simon."

"Then fetch your bonnet and cloak . . . quickly."

Li, moving through the jostling crowds in Piccadilly, suddenly saw a high-perch phaeton making its way through the press of traffic.

The couple in it looked very elegant and very much in love. The man driving was torn between keeping his attention on his horses and looking down into the pretty face of his companion.

With a start, Li recognized her ex-prisoner, and watched the glowing happiness of the couple with wide-eyed wonder.

I'm glad I didn't kill her, she said to herself, and went on her way, buoyed up by that generous thought which lasted for quite ten minutes.

We hope you have enjoyed this Large Print book. Other G.K. Hall & Co. or Chivers Press Large Print books are available at your library or directly from the publishers.

For more information about current and up-coming titles, please call or write, without obligation, to:

G.K. Hall & Co.
295 Kennedy Memorial Drive
Waterville, ME 04901
Tel. (800) 223-1244
Tel. (800) 223-6121

OR

Chivers Press Limited
Windsor Bridge Road
Bath BA2 3AX
England
Tel. (0225) 335336

All our Large Print titles are designed for easy reading, and all our books are made to last.

LP CHESNEY

Chesney, Marion.
Lady Lucy's lover : Marion
Chesney.